JANE AIRHEAD

Kay Woodward

First published in Great Britain
in 2009 by
Andersen Press Ltd
This Large Print edition published
by AudioGO Ltd 2011
by arrangement with
Andersen Press Ltd

ISBN 978 1405 664714

British Library Cataloguing in Publication Data available

Printed and bound in Great Britain by
CPI Antony Rowe, Chippenham and Eastbourne

For Woody – Rochester, Darcy and Clarkson, rolled into one

CHAPTER ONE

Rain. There was no way Charlotte was going out in *that*. She stared wistfully at the big, fat drops splattering wetly against her bedroom window. She couldn't understand why everyone kept banging on about global warming. It was global wetting they should be worried about.

She sighed, impatiently swiping her cuff across the misted glass. Outside, the dull, grey, pebble-dashed houses across the street looked duller and greyer than usual. It didn't even look like a seaside town in this weather. Add to that fading paintwork, alien-like satellite dishes and concrete gardens—not to mention a total lack of greenery—and Charlotte was left with a view so far removed from her ideal outlook that it wasn't funny. What she really wanted to see was the Yorkshire Dales. The wonderfully gothic Thornfield Hall. She'd give anything to be there, living the thrilling, dramatic, romantic and totally spellbinding life of Jane—

'Eeeearrrggghhhh!'

With a cry of anguish, Charlotte slipped off the edge of the tiny windowsill where she'd been crouching—scrabbling helplessly at the curtains as she fell—and landed in an undignified heap on the floor.

'Ooof,' she said belatedly, before carefully feeling for broken bones and reluctantly admitting to herself that there were none. Just as there was no Jane Eyre in this bedroom. Or this century.

But she could dream, right? If only she'd had enough room to do that dreaming. The real Jane Eyre had had a window seat as big as a surfboard on which to ponder her hard-done-by life. Charlotte had to make do with a plank of glossed four-by-two. There just wasn't the room to be a literary heroine in this house.

'Charlotte?' called her mother from downstairs.

'Yes, Mum?' she squeaked. Her head was squished against the radiator and growing uncomfortably hot.

'What did I tell you about balancing on that windowsill?'

'Not to . . .?' groaned Charlotte, rubbing her elbow. She'd ruined her authentic nineteenth-century hairdo too. It now hung in unruly, brown fronds around her face.

'You're far too old to be squeezing into hidey holes,' her mum continued, her voice growing louder as she climbed the stairs. 'You're very nearly fifteen.' She appeared at the door, leaned against the frame and looked down at her only daughter. A scathing expression battled with the smile tugging at one side of her mouth. But her eyes didn't even attempt to look cross—they twinkled like fairy lights.

'I was only reading—' began Charlotte.

'I know *exactly* what you were doing,' said her mum. 'Do you have to take that book quite so literally? Couldn't you just read on your bed like a normal teenager?'

'But—'

'I'm sorry. I know it must be

3

devastating to realise that you're not an unwanted, unloved orphan,' Mum went on, 'forced to read secretly on a hidden window seat in the house of cruel relatives who detest the air you breathe.' The corner of her mouth edged higher. 'But the trouble with Jane Eyre is that she's not real. And you are. You're my reasonably well-behaved, fairly bright and really quite lovely daughter. Although your hair could do with a trim,' she added.

Charlotte couldn't help sniggering. Her mum was the best.

'Shouldn't you be getting square eyes from watching too much television?' Mrs Penman asked. Once she got started on her favourite topic, it could be hours—literally—until she ran out of juice. 'How about cultivating an addiction to computer games? Running up a shocking mobile bill? Hanging around street corners with unsuitable boys?' She paused. 'Forget the last one.'

'My room's quite messy,' said Charlotte. 'Will that do?'

'I suppose so,' said Mum. Then she

was suddenly serious. 'All I'm saying is, there's more to life than books.'

'But you don't really believe that,' said Charlotte, unfolding her tangled limbs and struggling to her feet. 'You're an English teacher. You love metaphors and similes and past participles and . . . and . . . and syntax!' she finished triumphantly. 'You go ballistic if anyone breaks the spine of a book—even if doesn't belong to you!'

'Well . . . yes,' agreed her mum, with a theatrical shudder. This was totally true. Rumour had it that she'd once whipped a book out of an unsuspecting pupil's hands after they'd opened a paperback and—horror of horrors—wrenched back the covers so far that they touched. Mum insisted that the crack could be heard in London. Sixty miles away. 'But,' she added, 'some might argue that it's better to live life, instead of just reading about it. Or do both. That could work.'

Charlotte gave in gracefully, knowing that this particular rant had the potential to run as long as *Coronation Street*. 'How about I crinkle my hair with your old crimpers tonight—while you're marking homework—and smear on too much black eyeliner and go and be rebellious round at Manda's house? How does that sound?'

'Excellent,' her mum replied.

'Cool,' said Charlotte, opening her book once more. She might just have enough time to sigh dramatically over her favourite character's harrowing time at boarding school before tea.

'Oh, and sweetheart?' Her mum poked her head back round the door.

'Hmm?' said Charlotte, already lost.

'I didn't mean it about your bedroom,' said Mum. 'Do you think you could excavate the floor before you go out? It's weeks since I've seen your carpet.'

Charlotte sighed, listening to her mum's slippered feet padding back down the stairs. She shrugged at her reflection in the mirror. Unsurprisingly, and rather unhelpfully, her reflection shrugged back. She leaned closer and examined her face. Yep, it was still as nondescript as this morning. She had a complexion that beauty magazines flatteringly classed as 'sallow', meaning that in summer she was tanned and in winter she looked ill. Her hair was boringly brown, her eyes a muddy shade of greeny-brown and her nose far, far too big. She straightened up and her reflection shot out of sight. Hmmm . . . still as tall as this morning, too. If she really wanted to be Jane Eyre, who at best was petite and at worst, short, she'd seriously have to consider leg surgery. Or kneel.

Reluctantly, she tore herself away from the mirror and focused her attention on the surrounding chaos instead. The ancient wooden bookcase tilted dangerously under its wordy weight, and yellowing posters of squeaky-clean boy bands curled away from the wall. Magazines and school books coated the floor like the thick layers of marzipan and icing on a Christmas cake. Charlotte nibbled thoughtfully at the skin on the side of her thumb. Perhaps it *could* do with a bit of gentle bulldozing.

But in a room the size of Charlotte's,

tidying up was difficult. There wasn't enough space to fit a cat in—never mind swing it. She began to pick up random items one by one, contemplating how useful each was and whether she really needed it. After this important decision-making process, she chose either to jam things in her overflowing desk or simply put them back down again in another part of the room. As she rearranged the debris, she began to sort through her thoughts too.

Her mum was right. She could do with more thrills in her life. More *pzazz*. More *dazzle*. More ta-*daaaah*! But more *what*?

Most of the boys at school were uncultured berks who were too busy giving themselves repetitive strain injury of the iPod thumb. None of them glowered mysteriously with inner torment—although a few did have brilliantly glowing spots. And she was so tall that hardly any of them were much above shoulder height either. Whoever heard of a midget hero with acne and a skateboard?

There was the odd exception, of course. The delectable Jack Burley. Mmm . . . He was the totally cool class heart-throb with the chestnut-red hair, a complexion that glowed warmly even when he wasn't embarrassed and eyes as green as stagnant pond water. (Charlotte made a mental note to think up a better description when she was next in swoon mode.)

Yeah. Like he'd ever look twice at her.

No, until she found a boyfriend who could gaze into her eyes without the aid of stepladders and who knew the difference between a Brontë and a Brontosaurus, she'd have to look elsewhere for excitement.

And then it came to her.

There was a much more pressing problem to solve. Her *mum's* love life. She hadn't been near a bloke since the split. It wasn't that Mum was traumatised, far from it. Charlotte's parents had agreed that—with the exception of Charlotte herself, they were careful to point out to her—their marriage had been a terrible mistake and that they would be much happier apart. Will Penman spent much of the year abroad anyway, touring the Grand Prix circuits of the world. He worked for one of the smaller Formula One teams and counted himself one of the luckiest men alive to be wielding the stop-go sign in the pit lane every other Sunday. He'd only been run over once, he told Charlotte proudly. And a fractured metatarsal was a small price to pay for following his motor-racing dream.

Charlotte wasn't traumatised either, not really. She would have liked to be part of a nuclear family—once she realised that it meant old-fashioned rather than radioactive—but she and Mum made a great team. Her grandparents popped up with the regularity of weeds. And, as long as it was between the months of October and March or during the British Grand Prix, she got to see Dad every other weekend. The rest of the year, they emailed daily.

But she worried about Mum. Such a bubbly woman deserved a bloke—all the chick-lit novels said so. And that was where the Grand Plan came in. She, Charlotte Penman, aged fourteen, wannabe Jane Eyre, would find Mum her very own, dark, romantic and ever-so-enigmatic boyfriend. Her own Edward Fairfax Rochester! Naturally, she would make sure that Mum's perfect man didn't have as tortured a soul as Jane Eyre's hero. Instead, *her* Mr Rochester would be reliable and cool. He would have dark hair and dark eyes. He would be serious, yet charming, with a quirky sense of humour and a pair of magnificent sideburns.

In short, he would be perfect.

Charlotte would be shopping for that bridesmaid dress before she knew it.

CHAPTER TWO

'Oy!'

With the reflexes of a quick-witted TV cop, Charlotte swivelled her head left and right, before whirling round to glance back along the pavement. She gave a grin at the girl with 'cherry-red' tresses who was hurtling her way. They'd coloured her best friend's hair—and the towel and the bathroom carpet—last week. Personally, Charlotte thought it looked as brown as ever, but in certain lights and if you squinted in a special way, she supposed that there was a slight fruity glow. 'Manda!'

'So . . . what happened . . . to . . . you . . . last night?' puffed Manda, clattering to a halt beside her. Like most other people, she was shorter than Charlotte. Her eyes were baby blue and her nose was as petite as Charlotte's was huge.

'Oops!' Charlotte groaned. 'I totally forgot. You see, I was reading—'

'Let me guess,' interrupted Manda, as they walked onwards. 'You were reading *that book* for the gazillionth time and, because you knew the words so well, you were hypnotised and you spent the whole evening in a deadly trance that prevented you from lifting a finger to call your dearest friend and explain why you hadn't come round. As agreed. On the phone. Yesterday evening.'

'No, really!' protested Charlotte. 'I'm at the really fantastic bit where Jane becomes a teacher, but I tore myself away and—'

'Get *on* with it . . .' sighed Manda, who knew the story of *Jane Eyre* backwards thanks to Charlotte.

'And I had a totally top idea,' said Charlotte proudly. 'I'm going to sort out my mum's love life.'

'Does it *need* sorting out?' Manda asked. 'She always seems perfectly happy to me.'

'*Yes*,' said Charlotte with gusto. Since yesterday evening, the idea that her mum was in need of a bloke had leaped from pure speculation to concrete fact. 'She needs a dashing, mysterious man with a love of literature and an embarrassingly overpaid job to come and sweep her off her feet. And take her for posh meals and on holiday to exotic sun-kissed beaches. Oh, and visit museums without whingeing.'

13

'Shouldn't your mum be the one who's looking for this terrific guy?' asked Manda, perfectly reasonably.

'Ah . . .' said Charlotte.

Manda raised an eyebrow.

'I've worked it all out,' said Charlotte, whose Grand Plan had now gained the momentum of a runaway train. 'She isn't looking for this Mr Fantastic because she's too concerned about the effect it would have on me. She doesn't want to upset my schooling, what with the exams coming up, and she thinks that a third person in our household would upset the dynamics.'

Manda's eyebrow shot up even higher. (She had a very flexible face.) 'The exams that you'll be taking in two years?'

Charlotte nodded.

'And how do you know that she's not already looking for this Mr Fantastic?'

'Because she would already have found him by now,' said Charlotte logically. 'Look at the evidence: she's not bad-looking; she can change the oil in a car; she can make profiteroles.

14

Why wouldn't she have found her perfect man if it weren't for me and my wellbeing?'

Manda put her head on one side. 'So it's *not* because you want to be a bridesmaid?'

Charlotte did her best to look as if the idea had never occurred to her. Then she lost her battle against the blush that flooded her cheeks. 'Well, if that was what Mum wanted, I *suppose* that I could be persuaded,' she said. 'I wouldn't wear peach, though. Or pink or orange or lilac or lime green. And I don't want ruffles. And definitely no sweetheart neckline.' Charlotte shook her head sadly. She'd seen too many good friends humiliated in this way. 'Really, though, I just want my mum to be happy.' And she did. The perfect bridesmaid's dress was just a bonus. She tried out the beseeching look she'd been practising. 'Will you help?'

Manda folded her arms. Charlotte couldn't decide whether she looked more like a politician, a teacher or a traffic warden. Whatever, Manda was going to make a really good grown-up

15

one day. Then she smiled. ' 'Course I will!'

'Woo!' Charlotte didn't realise how anxious she'd been until she relaxed. This was great news.

'So, what happens next?' asked Manda.

'That's easy,' replied Charlotte, heaving her bulging bag further up on her shoulder. 'It's Monday, it's five to nine . . . it's assembly with Miss Scatcherd.'

Manda sighed. 'You mean Miss Stone,' she said. 'When I last checked, we weren't being beaten to a pulp in the nineteenth century. In *Jane Eyre*.'

Charlotte bit her lip. She really must try harder to remember what was real and what wasn't. The men in white coats would take her away if she kept mixing up fact and fiction. And then who would make her mum's life complete?

*　　　*　　　*

As the last of the pupils filed into the hall, the jangling, jarring sounds of

16

Mr Jeffries's piano faded away.

'Is it over?' whispered Manda, carefully pulling her fingers out of her ears. 'When are they going to tune that piano? Don't they realise that it's highly upsetting for someone as musical as myself to have to listen to such—'

'Shhhh!' Scarlet-lipsticked Mrs Hook glared menacingly and Charlotte wondered anew how her form teacher could do such a lifelike impression of a pantomime dame.

As if sensing her thoughts, Mrs Penman's head snapped round. With pursed lips, the English teacher glared towards them. Her gaze settled on her daughter and she frowned fiercely, before turning back to the front.

Charlotte felt a wave of guilt wash over her. Sometimes—like now, for instance—she wished her mum had chosen a different career. Celebrity journalism would be ideal, but any job that didn't require Charlotte to behave at school would do the trick. It wasn't that she was an aspiring hooligan, just that she'd have liked the option to be

17

reckless and daring if she felt like it.

She slumped down in her plastic chair and raised her eyes ceiling-wards. Nothing ever seemed to change around here. Same old badly tuned piano . . . same old extra-vigilant teachers . . . same old Isle-of-Wight-shaped crack in the paintwork—

'*Morning!*' boomed Miss Stone, her voice slicing through Charlotte's thoughts like a hot knife through low-fat buttery spread.

The chatter that bubbled and rattled around the hall ceased at once. No one ever tried to compete with the head teacher. It was rumoured that locals in the surrounding streets left the area before assembly began. On sports day, it was said that the whole town was evacuated.

The pupils weren't so lucky.

'MORNING!' repeated Miss Stone.

'*Mor*-ning-Miss-*Sto-wone*,' chanted the pupils.

'Splendid!' shouted the head teacher, her smooth helmet of steel-grey hair moving perfectly in time as she nodded her head. 'Now, I have a

18

number of notices this morning.'

Charlotte went back to staring at the ceiling as the daily tirade kicked off.

'Firstly, I am disappointed to learn that the marvellous new statue of the school's founder has been dressed up as a Manchester United player. The football fan that kindly donated the strip may come to my office to claim it back—along with five detentions.' Miss Stone scanned the sea of pupils. 'If I don't hear anything by three thirty, the outfit goes to Oxfam.'

There was a sharp gasp near the back of the assembly hall.

Miss Stone smiled smugly and then continued. 'Secondly, I'd like to remind you that unsuitable earrings are strictly prohibited, as are all nose-rings, lip-rings, eyebrow-rings and navel-rings. Anyone found on school premises with decorated, punctured flesh'– the head teacher paused as everyone sucked air between their teeth—'will be suspended with immediate effect. It's time to ring the changes around here.'

The pupils looked blank.

'*Ring* the changes?' repeated Miss

Stone loudly. Then she sighed and went on to the next item on her agenda.

The head teacher boomed and wailed through her usual list of rebukes and warnings—anyone found modifying the school uniform would be flogged, anyone found faking early-dinner passes would be put in solitary confinement . . . Or something like that. Blah, blah, blinking blah.

'And now, time for some rather pleasant news,' bellowed the head teacher.

'Yeah—right,' whispered Manda.

'I'm delighted to introduce a new . . .'

'Public holiday?' mumbled Charlotte.

'Series of exams for Year 9, I'll bet,' said Manda.

'Shhhh!' hissed three teachers in unison.

'. . . member of staff!' finished Miss Stone proudly.

A buzz of excitement zinged round the hall. This really *was* news.

Charlotte and Manda exchanged

glances and then set about scanning the teachers dotted around the hall.

Where . . .? Who . . .? *Well, hell-o!*

Charlotte sat bolt upright. There, to the left of the stage, on the end of a row of crushingly normal teachers, lounged a real, true-life Mr Fantastic. No tweed jacket, no elbow patches, no snagged beige trousers. And not a tasselled loafer in sight.

Instead, the new teacher was dark—dark hair, dark skin and dark arched eyebrows—with a brooding, impenetrable expression that was straight out of the pages of The Book.

Charlotte's mouth hung open in disbelief. The answer to her prayers had been delivered straight into her lap. This was a new man for her mum. This was—

'This is our new French teacher,' roared Miss Stone gaily. 'Mr Grant, I'd like to introduce you to the pupils of Harraby Comprehensive School.'

He was perfect.

CHAPTER THREE

Charlotte had changed her mind about Mr Grant. Completely. Utterly. Categorically. In fact, there weren't enough words in the school library's 1993 edition of the Shorter Oxford Dictionary—which was the *longest* dictionary she'd ever seen—to describe how much Charlotte detested the new teacher.

It had all started very badly and gone downhill from there.

This term, Charlotte's timetable read like something out of a horror film. If she hadn't known for a fact that the school's purpose was to educate her, while simultaneously transforming her into a well-rounded person, admirably equipped with all the skills needed to cope in the Real World—or so her mum had told her—then she might have thought that this was a heavily disguised torture chamber.

Monday was by far the worst day of the week. The day started with Art.

(Pablo Picasso's dog was more artistic than Charlotte.) It continued with PE. (Charlotte was as stiff as a board.) After lunch, it was Science. (Charlotte and Bunsen burners were an explosive combination.) But, after the hours of torment, Charlotte's day was topped off with French—one of her favourite subjects.

Until now, that was.

During the break before French, Charlotte's friends had worked themselves up into a crescendo of excitement. New teachers didn't start at Harraby Comp every term. Good-looking teachers were like gold dust. The girls argued over who had the biggest crush on the gorgeous Mr Grant. The boys were more laid-back—and rather disappointed that the glamorous Madame Bertillon had returned to her native France, taking her size eight clothes and pert bottom with her.

Meanwhile, Charlotte had far more important things on her mind. She quickly went through her Grand Plan, which she'd been tweaking since that morning's assembly.

1. Assess candidate's suitability for husband and—ultra important—stepdad role in Penman household.
2. If candidate scores highly, introduce to potential wife.
3. Choose material for bridesmaid's dress.

It was too easy for words. Charlotte couldn't *wait* to get cracking. She took a deep, calming yogic breath, focused her mind and, at the first ting of the bell, she strode purposefully out of the concrete yard and towards Mr Grant's room, where, laughing, jostling and—in some cases—punching each other, the pupils crammed themselves through the doorway and made their way to their usual seats.

Automatically, Charlotte logged Jack Burley's position—three desks to the right and two rows back—before dumping her exercise books onto her desk. Even though she knew he'd never look twice at her, she liked to know

24

where he was. 'This is going to be so cool!' she exclaimed to anyone within earshot.

'Really?' said Julia Williams, who claimed to be aloof from the charms of Mr Grant on the grounds that she had a crush on the History teacher instead.

'Really,' insisted Charlotte, nodding excitedly. 'Cool sideburns, cool clothes . . . how could he be anything other than a totally cool teacher?'

Around her, the room fell silent.

'I'm glad you think so,' said a low voice, edged with sarcasm.

Charlotte knew without looking who had arrived. And she also knew that this wasn't a terrific way to kick-start her mum's new relationship. She clenched her teeth into an uncomfortable grimace and swivelled slowly on one heel to face the music.

Mr Grant was lolling in the chair at the front of the classroom. He glared at Charlotte. 'Your name?'

'Shhh . . .' said Charlotte nervously.

Mr Grant arched an eyebrow. 'Young lady—you seem to be confused about the teacher-pupil *status quo* in a classroom situation,' he said. 'I'll do any shushing that is required.'

Mark Cooper spluttered, stopping mid-snigger when Jack Burley poked him with a ruler.

'Shhh-arlotte.' She squeezed out the rest of her name like toothpaste from an almost-empty tube.

'Hmmm.' Mr Grant made a note in his register and looked up. 'Charlotte, as you're so well versed in the subject, perhaps you'd like to tell me—and the rest of the class—why sideburns are a prerequisite to good teaching. In French, of course.'

A wave of giggles rolled around the classroom.

Charlotte gulped and cleared her throat. She looked around frantically for support and, wide-eyed, Manda stared back at her. Great. Her best friend was going to be as much help as a Russian phrase book in Wales.

'Um . . . errr . . .' Charlotte began, shrugging her shoulders dramatically. 'Er . . . *monsieur* . . .' She started to feel more confident. This was going well, she could feel it. All she needed was an egg cup of French paint-stripper coffee and she'd look the part, totally. '*Mais*—'

'Get *on* with it, Miss Penman!' barked Mr Grant.

'*Les sideburns sont magnifiques*!' she gabbled.

There was silence for a millisecond, before laughter exploded all around.

One glowering stare from the French teacher brought silence.

'Hardly an adequate explanation,' Mr Grant said dismissively. He turned his attention to the rest of the class and Charlotte took the opportunity to slide into her seat and sink as low as she could go. 'Now, before Ofsted inspectors parachute in to investigate the lack of teaching taking place in this classroom, I suggest that we explore the mysteries of the subjunctive tense.'

Charlotte watched glumly as the French teacher glowered and frowned and simmered at the front of the classroom. He still *looked* like a romantic hero, but now she knew better. He was just plain mean.

Jane Eyre had had it tough, no

question. Miserable Mr Rochester was one of the sternest and grumpiest heart-throbs of all time. (He wasn't much of a looker either—although Charlotte privately spiced up his appearance with a sprinkling of Depp and a smidgen of Pitt.) But the new French teacher took the biscuit for sheer crossness. Charlotte suddenly had visions of Mr Grant stomping bad-temperedly down the aisle with her mum . . . Mr Grant banishing her to her room for extra homework . . . Mr Grant handing her a cloth to wipe off make-up . . . She could feel her Grand Plan disintegrating around her.

Did her mum deserve this? More to the point, did *Charlotte*?

*   *   *

'I don't think it went too badly,' said Manda kindly as they escaped through the school gates.

'Are you kidding?' Charlotte groaned. 'It's a disaster! I picked the most charmless and pompous person *ever* to marry my poor, dear mother.

What was I thinking? Just because she's a teacher and Jane Eyre was a governess doesn't mean that they'll both get on with crotchety, grouchy, charmless—'

'You already said that,' said Manda. 'How about miserable?'

'Grrrrrr,' growled Charlotte. 'For Brontë's sake, I'm named after the woman who wrote *Jane Eyre*! I of all people should be able to find a romantic hero for Mum and stage-manage a simple wedding. What's so difficult about that?' With a theatrical flourish, she ran her hand through her hair, instantly snagging her fingers in the mass of tangled curls.

Manda nodded understandingly. 'I think you're forgetting something,' she said.

'What?' Charlotte mumbled crossly, extricating her fingers and trying to swirl her hair into a stunning, yet low-maintenance style at the same time. It was no good. She'd have to go for her usual hairdo: a right state.

'Several somethings, actually,' said Manda, springing into action as the

Voice of Reason. She splayed out the fingers of her left hand and began to count them off with her—very stern—right forefinger. 'One—you're not meant to be falling in love with him, your mum is. Two—you got his attention, and any publicity is good publicity. Three—he's hardly going to start auditioning for the role of stepdad in front of a panel of thirty pupils. Four—you redeemed yourself in that spoddy aural comprehension test he did.'

'I did all right, didn't I?' said Charlotte, scrunching up her mouth. She wasn't good at 'bigging herself up' as Manda put it. 'And at least I didn't get *aural* and *oral* mixed up on purpose, like the boys. They got much more of a ticking off than me.' She smiled. This was brilliant—she was feeling better by the plus point. 'Five?' she added hopefully.

'Nope, that's your lot,' said Manda briskly. 'Besides, you don't *need* any more reasons to realise that things aren't so bad.'

Charlotte nodded cautiously. Mr

Grant might be in dire need of a humour transplant, but Mr Rochester was hardly a stand-up comedian. So perhaps she didn't need to wave goodbye to her dreams of a sophisticated bridesmaid's dress just yet.

Unbidden, a soft-focus vision popped into her head, in which she was rugby-tackling a fellow bridesmaid for possession of the wedding bouquet, while Jack Burley cheered her on.

Briskly, she banished the image to the back of her mind. What was she doing thinking of Jack at a time like this?

She must concentrate on Mr Grant.

He was the important one.

CHAPTER FOUR

'I've joined a new book group,' announced Mum the next morning, as she merrily drowned the half-dead basil plant before plonking it back on the windowsill to fend for itself for another week.

'Cool,' gurgled Charlotte, through a mouthful of muesli. She didn't bother to lift her head from *Jane Eyre* because this was nothing new. Her mum was *always* joining book groups . . . and leaving them in high dudgeon when she disagreed with the choice of book. She'd been a member of three at the last count. At the same time. The thought of so much enforced reading made Charlotte's eyes go all blurry.

There was Mum's highbrow book group, which discussed horribly clever books with thin pages and small writing. Charlotte wasn't even sure that her mum enjoyed it and suspected that she only went for form's sake. Her lowbrow book group talked about fun books, but not fat books with gold writing on the cover, because Mrs Penman absolutely drew the line there. She had standards, as she told her daughter on a regular basis. Whatever they talked about in the third book group, it certainly wasn't books, because Charlotte had overheard them when it was Mum's turn to host. There seemed to be a lot of giggling and a tremendous amount of red wine involved, but not a single mention of *Jane Eyre*, which made it utterly pointless as far as she was concerned.

'So I'll be going tonight,' said Mum, popping a sweetener into her coffee.

'Hmm?' Charlotte had already drifted back to Thornfield.

Mum tutted. 'The book group. Tonight. Seven o'clock. You'll be OK on your own for a couple of hours, won't you?' She aimed a splash of milk at her cup and missed, spattering the worktop instead.

Charlotte hadn't believed that her mum could get any clumsier, but apparently she'd been wrong. 'No problem,' she said, turning her attention back to her book. . . back to the gloomy drawing room where Rochester was interrogating Jane. She couldn't help thinking that if he hadn't decided to be a flawed romantic hero, he could have been a teacher instead.

'And you won't—'

Charlotte looked up blearily, automatic replies at the ready. 'Play with knives? No.' Her mum's questions were nothing if not predictable.

'Or—'

'Reveal personal details in online chatrooms? I'm not daft, Mum.'

'But you might want to—'

'Yes, I'll phone Grandma and Grandad,' said Charlotte. 'Aren't they coming down soon?'

Mum nodded. 'Next month.'

'Cool.'

It was impossible to concentrate on The Book while Mum was in this sort of mood. Charlotte closed it with a snap. 'So what are you reading?'

'Hmm?'

Charlotte sighed. Parents could be amazingly contrary. One minute they wanted your full, undivided attention. The next, they were visiting Cloud Cuckoo Land. 'Which book are you reading?' she repeated. And then, when there was no response, 'For the book group?'

'Oh, we haven't decided yet,' mumbled Mum, who'd developed a sudden interest in the inner lining of her briefcase. Then, without warning, she shot to her feet like a jack-in-the-box. 'Are you ready to go? I'll drop you off if you get a wriggle on!' She said it as if getting to school early was a good thing.

Charlotte smiled to herself. She didn't have to be a rocket scientist to work out what was going on. The real reason why Mum was so eager to leave early was to give her bonus time for flirting with the new French teacher in the staff room. As for this supposed book group . . . Charlotte seriously doubted its existence. It was simply an elaborate ruse to allow Mum to go out for drinks, food or whatever it was that forty-somethings did when they were too old for clubbing. Her companion for the evening? Mr Grant, of course.

She didn't fool Charlotte one bit.

*   *   *

Mum tip-tapped down the path in her kitten heels a little after seven, leaving Charlotte to contemplate a whole evening to herself. After a brief interlude spent yelping in agony as she plucked her eyebrows, she checked her email. There were two messages waiting for her, the first from Dad, who was in Italy this week.

To: janeeyre2@gmail.com
From: formulafantastic@hotmail.com
Subject: Monza

Hi pet!
Doing OK? I'm great, though my bald spot is worrying me. Seems to be getting bigger. Might need to polish it soon. Tough week ahead. New tyres are giving us trouble and the drivers have got the hump as per blinking usual. Look out for me on telly?
Dad X
PS Want any cheese?

Charlotte bashed out a quick reply. Epic emails scared her dad. Chances are, he'd worry so much about having to write a long reply that he'd never get round to doing it.

To: formulafantastic@hotmail.com
From: janeeyre2@gmail.com

Subject: Re: Monza

Hi Dad!
I'm great. Wear a hat. Hope the race goes well—remember to stand out of the way before the driver sets off.
Charlotte xxxxx
PS Parmesan, please. The proper stuff, not those sicky crumbs.

It was History the next morning. For once it was riveting. Charlotte happily immersed herself in the Industrial Revolution. Coal, candles, consumption . . . It was all very romantic in a thank-heavens-she-didn't-actually-have-to-live-then-like-the-Brontës-did sort of way. Charlotte scribbled down copious notes about seed drills and cotton mills, feeling so close to her favourite author that she could smell the cholera.

'Hey, Chas—what's with the bionic pen?' scoffed Jack Burley after the lesson, grinning over at his mates to indicate that a moment of comedy perfection was taking place. They beamed back obligingly. Not only was

37

Jack popular with the girls, he was considered one of the lads too, a truly exalted position to be in.

'Huh?' said Charlotte, lost in a world of her own. 'Bionic? No, it's a Bic, stupid.'

'Er, yeah . . . I knew that,' mumbled Jack. 'I was just, er . . . Hey, lads, fancy a game of footie?' He pushed back his floppy fringe, grabbed his ball-shaped rucksack and hastily flung it over his shoulder, before sauntering away.

'Did you see that?' gasped Manda.

'What?' said Charlotte, looking blank.

'Jack,' said Manda. And then, when there was no response, 'Jack Burley. He spoke to you.'

'Yep,' replied Charlotte, leafing through her exercise book to check the proximity of cotton mills to Haworth, the home of her heroine. 'And?'

'Have you totally lost the plot?'

'Have I what . . .?' said Charlotte. Suddenly, she was hot with embarrassment. 'Oh.'

'Oh, indeed.'

'Jack Burley,' repeated Charlotte

38

slowly, realising that not only had she given the best-looking boy in the class the brush-off, she'd also called him 'stupid'. And—the worst sin of all—she'd performed her anti-seduction routine in front of his friends, thereby making him look a pillock too.

Charlotte gave Manda a wonky smile. 'Hey, it's not the end of the world,' she lamented, knowing quite well that it was. 'It's not like I ever stood a chance with him, is it? And what sort of a nickname is Chas anyway . . . ?'

Manda shook her head in despair. 'Come on,' she said. 'We have a date with the lunch queue. You don't want to miss out on that too.'

*   *   *

By the time they reached the dining hall, the noise was amazing. A percussion of tinkling cutlery and crashing trays accompanied a babble of voices. Everyone—pupils, teachers, dinner ladies—seemed to be doing their collective best to make as much racket as possible.

Charlotte and Manda lunged for the most appetising meals on offer—it wasn't a difficult choice—and escaped to a sparsely populated corner of the hall, the only spot where earplugs weren't required.

The vegetable lasagne was pretty good though. It almost made up for the lack of burgers and turkey twizzlers. What it *didn't* make up for was the gaping chip-shaped hole on the food counter. They'd been just there, to the left of the mung beans. Charlotte sighed longingly at their banishment to the World of Food That is Bad For You by TV Chefs Who Know What is Best For You. Then her eyes were drawn to two teachers on the far side of the dining hall. They were nudging their trays along the food counter, pausing only to point to a steaming dish . . . and to gaze lovingly at each other.

It was her mum and Mr Grant.

Yay!

CHAPTER FIVE

Charlotte was seriously contemplating going for an eye test. Apparently, her mum had *so* not been staring lovingly into the gorgeous Mr Grant's eyes. She'd been staring at him, yes. But only because she was dumbstruck by what the handsome French teacher was saying.

'He was unbelievable!' stormed Mrs Penman that evening, slamming a saucepan onto the hob and glugging in olive oil. Shaking her head, she wrenched open the fridge door and began pulling random vegetables from the shelves, which she flung onto the worktop as if they were hand grenades. A bright spot of colour burned high on each cheekbone—she was *very* angry.

Charlotte sagged against the doorframe. She'd been so looking forward to hearing these words, but hadn't imagined that they'd be spoken with such venom. Why? She didn't think Mr Grant had been too bad, lately. In the last couple of lessons, he'd only criticised her pronunciation three times. She'd even got a *bien* for her essay about French strikes. 'What did he do?' she ventured.

'Do? *Do*!' said her mum. 'He didn't *do* anything! It's what he *said*.'

'Right,' said Charlotte, peeping furtively at her watch and wondering if Mum was going to spill the beans this side of midnight. She'd hoped to squeeze in a quick chapter before *EastEnders*.

After chopping an onion at dizzying—and rather terrifying—speed, before hurling the tiny pieces of decimated vegetable into the saucepan, Mum turned to face her bemused daughter. 'He *said* that I should stick to teaching English and not interfere in the inner workings of his department. *That's* what he said. Can you believe that someone could be so *rude*?'

'Oh.' Charlotte swallowed. These were hardly the words of a potential suitor. Or even the words of a potential acquaintance. 'And what did you say to him?' she said.

Bang! Mum thumped the heel of her hand onto her knife, crushing a blameless clove of garlic into pulp. She casually stripped off the outer husk, before scraping the squished remnants into a saucepan. 'I told him that there was no need to be so waspish,' she said haughtily.

Waspish? Charlotte tutted to herself. Mum had obviously been at the Austen again.

Charlotte edged her way round the kitchen towards the larder. Tugging a can of chopped tomatoes from the shelf, she set to work with the tin opener. She knew from long experience that whenever Mum was especially wound up she cooked pasta and tomato sauce. There was something calming about the whole chopping and stirring process, apparently. Not that you'd know it, the way she was wielding that kitchen knife. Her mother seemed to have morphed into a grumpy teenager. Charlotte tried again, feeling like the grown-up for once. 'I meant, what did you say *before* he was so rude?'

Her mum sniffed. Whether it was because of the sizzling onions or for the loss of her future spouse, Charlotte wasn't sure. 'All I did was explain to him some of the school's procedures,' Mum said, her voice as sharp as her knife. She sniffed again. It was definitely the onions.

Charlotte nodded. She didn't need a crystal ball to see which way this was heading.

'I mean, he's new, isn't he?' continued Mum. 'How is he to know basic school procedures?'

Charlotte leaned against the fridge and waited patiently for the rest of the details. She was sure they wouldn't be long in coming.

They weren't.

'And I said that I'd heard his last school was rather rough and warned him that we were expecting an Ofsted inspection later this term,' said Mum. 'I offered to look over his lesson plans if he needed any pointers.'

'That's all?' asked Charlotte.

'Nearly,' said Mum, looking less sure of herself now. 'I might have mentioned how highly Madame Bertillon had always scored with the inspectors . . . but I told him not to worry because the French department was bound to do well this time too, as long as he put the hours in.' She plucked a jar of oregano from a shelf and waved it above the bubbling saucepan. A shower of green flakes cascaded through the air.

'Let me guess,' said Charlotte. 'He was offended?'

'Er, yes,' said her mum. She turned to her daughter and smiled ruefully, her anger spent. 'I was only trying to be helpful . . . Did it sound like I was sticking my nose in?'

'Honestly?' asked Charlotte, wrinkling her nose. A waft of pasta sauce flooded her senses and made her stomach growl.

Mum nodded.

'Well, I'd give you eleven out of ten for helpfulness . . .' she said cautiously. 'But do you think you might have come across a tiny bit bossy?'

'I stuck my nose in . . .' Mum sighed. 'Me and my big nose.' She meant it.

Charlotte wasn't the only one to have a whopping hooter.

'Well, perhaps it wasn't *that* bad,' said Charlotte, knowing that it was.

'It was,' said her mum firmly, pouring pasta twists into bubbling water and stirring. Her spoon slowed. 'But never mind. Mr Grant and I teach different subjects. Our classrooms are at opposite ends of the school. It shouldn't be *too* difficult to avoid him. And if ever we meet up, I shall maintain a totally professional relationship. It's not as if we were ever good friends, is it?'

Pop! The fragile bubble that held Charlotte's bridesmaid's dress burst and wisps of cappuccino silk floated gently away.

*   *   *

Later that evening, Charlotte twisted the cap off the Tippex and painted out the totally ridiculous sentence she'd just written. Her new career of matchmaking was playing havoc with her homework, especially now that everything had gone belly-up.

She was alone in the house. Strangely, and utterly pointlessly, Mum had gone to her fictitious book group after all. Charlotte didn't know why. There was no need for pretence now, not once the date with Mr Grant had been cancelled. Because it *must* have been cancelled, not unless the warring teachers had planned to kick box by candlelight. Still, Charlotte was going along with the charade, wondering what her jilted mother would do for the evening while she was pretending to be discussing the latest McEwan with her imaginary literary friends.

Charlotte pondered the facts. And it didn't look good. Her mum and Mr Grant had offended each other. They hated each other. They were like . . . they were like . . . olive oil and balsamic vinegar!

Despite the crushing disappointment of her failed matchmaking, Charlotte couldn't help congratulating herself on the *rightness* of this analogy. She'd once tried to make salad dressing—her grandparents had been visiting and they *loved* salad—but no matter how long or how violently she'd shaken the jam jar of oil and vinegar, as soon as she stopped, the dark droplets of balsamic vinegar had sunk, while the silky oil gracefully rose to the surface. They just didn't mix.

Charlotte scratched her head thoughtfully. Should she give up on Mr Grant as a future stepfather before she'd even properly begun her matchmaking campaign? All the evidence pointed towards one matrimonial-busting conclusion: it was a match made in hell.

Or was it?

Because there was something about olive oil and balsamic vinegar that Charlotte had forgotten. They might not mix, but the two tastes worked perfectly together . . . Or so her posh grandparents said, anyway.

CHAPTER SIX

Charlotte rubbed her hand thoughtfully across her chin and squeaked 'Ow!' as she encountered yet another mountainous spot. It was her third this week—her third! What was going on?! The worst school nickname of all loomed large. Pizza face. Arrrggghhh!

Charlotte quickly flicked through her latest magazine and checked out the Spot Advice section, to make sure that it hadn't magically changed since last time she looked at it. It hadn't.

Under no circumstances should you squeeze spots, said Dr Maud primly. *This will make them much, much worse. Instead, keep the area spotlessly clean . . .*

Was she trying to be funny? Spotlessly? Ha ha.

. . . and within a few days . . .

A few days? She didn't have a few days! She'd be a social leper *long* before a few days were over.

. . . the inflamed area will have

subsided and your skin will be soft and as good as new.

Either Dr Maud had never had a spot in her life or she actively liked being a human domino. Charlotte didn't. And there was little point coating the offending pustule with a layer of concealer. It didn't matter whether they were pillar-box red, sunny yellow or beige—a spot was a spot whichever way you looked at it.

After a quick pit stop in the bathroom to lather up to her elbows and rinse clean, Charlotte marched back to her room, holding dripping hands aloft. Well, that was how surgeons did it on telly before performing surgery, so she knew that it must be right.

A poke and a—supremely satisfying—squeeze later, it was all over. Charlotte breathed a sigh of relief.

Now, where was she? Ah, yes.

Charlotte flipped open her notebook and grasped a pen. She was going to assess the current situation calmly, clearly, objectively and with no messing.

1. Mum is persisting with her fantasy book group, even going so far as telling me she'd be reading *The Time Traveler's Wife* next. A cunning ruse, but pathetically predictable. That is what *all* book groups read.
2. Mum and Mr Grant are maintaining a truly professional relationship. (I know this for a fact. I've seen them expertly ignoring each other across a crowded room.)
3. Jack Burley hasn't spoken to me since I called him 'stupid'.

Oh.

Charlotte wasn't quite sure how the last point had crept in and scored it out crossly. Several times. Whatever Jack Burley thought of her wasn't relevant to the Grand Plan. Her objectives were to secure her mum's happiness. She didn't have the time or the resources to convince the coolest lad in school with the flippy-floppy hair that not only did she *not* hate him, but that he was madly in love with *her*. No, she had to remain focused.

Although he did have the most extraordinary green eyes . . . not stagnant pond water, but the colour of that wheatgrass juice that she'd once gulped down in a fit of health-consciousness. Charlotte screwed up her face and shivered involuntarily as she remembered just how grim it had tasted. Urgh. She scrabbled around for the perfect description. Were Jack's eyes more like Brussels sprouts? Nope. Again, her taste buds rebelled. Ah . . . Now she had it. The skin of an avocado! The dark green outer shell wasn't something that she'd ever tasted, but it held the promise of cool, creamy avocado flesh.

Charlotte snorted loudly at her inability to liken Jack Burley's eyes to anything more romantic than a vegetable. She blamed her mum for this. If Mrs Penman hadn't put in a regular order for an organic vegetable box, neither of them would be so obsessed with the stuff.

It went like this. Every Wednesday, the delivery man left a small cardboard box—recycled, of course—beside the back door. When she got in from school, Charlotte lugged the box onto the kitchen table, but she didn't dare open it. To her mum, this was an offence on a par with Ruining the Punchline of a Good Novel.

As soon as Mum arrived home, Charlotte made her a cup of camomile tea, although she honestly didn't see the point. What was the difference between that and cloudy rainwater? Then she hung around nonchalantly to see what strange specimens she'd be eating that week, although the vegetables themselves weren't usually much of a clue, being ugly, knobbly things for the most part. And she wasn't sure whether Mum had much more of an idea than her, even though Mrs Penman confidently announced what was a celeriac and what was a cabbage. (Though even a vegetable-phobe like Charlotte could work that one out.) It was at this point that Mum started tugging books off her cookery shelf like a crazed librarian. Before long, she would be leafing through recipe books with reckless abandon, hunting frenziedly for meals that included the week's weird veg. It would be only a matter of minutes before curious phrases like *'celeri rémoulade'* and *'mushrooms à la grecque'* were whizzing past Charlotte's ears—and not much longer before the meals themselves were hovering on a fork before her suspicious eyes.

Reluctantly, Charlotte reminded herself that she wasn't a bumbling old MP who couldn't stick to the point and she swiftly concluded her inner ramblings: Mum *so* needed her help. If she could make such a meal—ha!—of a simple vegetable box, then how could she be trusted to find herself a man?

Charlotte knew what she had to do—and it wasn't going to be easy. *Très difficile*, as Mr Grant might say. *Impossible*, probably. She had to convince her mum that the dark, brooding, rather rude French teacher was just the man for her. And she had to convince Mr Grant that her mum wasn't an interfering busybody. She had to convince them to make up. And soon.

There was *nothing* more embarrassing than a bridesmaid with wrinkles.

CHAPTER SEVEN

Like a round cheese rolled from the top of a grassy hill, the autumn term began to gather speed. The new timetable became old and familiar and, although Monday's French lessons weren't ever going to be *formidable* with a capital *F*, Charlotte found that she was slowly growing used to Mr Grant's acerbic manner. To avoid being on the receiving end herself, the dog *never* ate her homework. She handed it in on time and got marks good enough to avoid the never-ending supply of dry—yet annoyingly witty— comments that the teacher doled out to the unluckier pupils. And apart from sneaking quick glances at Jack's lovely, chestnutty head as he bent over his textbooks, she avoided him too. Better that than make a fool of herself. She answered enough of Mr Grant's barked questions in class to prove that she was paying attention, but not so many that it looked like she was showing off. She was biding her time, waiting for just the right moment to further her romantic cause. Her mum's romantic cause, that was. Because Charlotte didn't have one. Definitely not.

And then came the perfect opportunity.

'If you could pass these onto your parents and impress upon them how much we are looking forward to their company,' said Mrs Hook during one Monday's registration, 'that would be wonderful. Do take care not to *lose* these letters,' she added meaningfully, her lipsticky smile fading. 'Otherwise, your parents won't be able to *sign and return the enclosed acceptance slips by the date indicated*, will they?'

There was a chorus of disappointed tuts as the pupils realised there was no way out.

Charlotte, on the other hand, was quietly pleased. She ran her fingertips over the white envelope, a Good Idea forming in her mind. A Remarkably Good Idea, in fact. So good that it very nearly blotted out the spectre of Parents' Evening.

Here was a golden opportunity for her mother and Mr Grant to set their difficulties aside and talk about something worthwhile.

Like Charlotte, for instance.

They were sure to bond, whether in mutual delight at her talent for rolling French Rs or horror at her inability to conjugate pluperfect verbs (a tongue-lashing she was quite prepared to suffer in the cause of true love). And, before long, they would doubtless be making arrangements to discuss the matter further over a nice bottle of red. It was almost too easy.

*   *   *

'Come on, hand it over.' Mrs Penman's voice was mock stern. 'I know you have it.'

With a flourish, Charlotte pulled the letter—or invitation to dinner, as she had begun to regard it—from her pocket and presented it solemnly to her mother. 'Don't forget to sign the slip,' she said. 'I don't want to get into trouble at school, do I?'

'Cheeky,' said Mum, scissoring her fingers along the envelope and pulling out the letter. She scanned it quickly before concluding, 'Well, isn't that just typical.'

Charlotte gulped. 'What?' she asked nervously. Had the school decided to whet parents' appetites in an attempt to boost attendance? She could just imagine it . . .

Join us for a night of embarrassing revelations!
Minx or mastermind? Find out what your child's *really* been up to!
You *believed* them when they said they were doing homework? Fool!
Whose child says 'nucular' instead of 'nuclear'? (Oh, the shame!)
All this and more [and quite possibly less] in the school hall on

Wednesday at 7pm.
You'd be a fool to miss it!

Charlotte shuddered.

'It's nothing really,' said Mum in a tone that implied that of all things it might be, it clearly *wasn't* nothing. 'It's my fault. I *knew* when parents' evening was, but I clean forgot. I can get out of it.'

'Get out of *what*?' said Charlotte.

The answer was unexpected. 'It's the same night as the book group, that's all.'

'Which new book group?' said Charlotte quickly, on the alert at once. Surely not the make-believe one? Didn't her mum know when to quit? Or—her spirits leaped—was it an ill-thought-out cover for a dinner arrangement? Had the two teachers made up without consulting their personal matchmaker?

'The new one.' Her mum laughed guiltily. 'I'm sure I said. It's no big deal. They're running one at the bookshop and a few of us from school thought we'd join. It makes a change from marking, you know. Even teachers need a break. We work *very* hard.'

She was making far, far too many excuses. Meanwhile, a warm glow was illuminating Mrs Penman's cheeks more effectively than any blusher. Flustered, she turned away and began sweeping the kitchen table clean of crumbs, tipping them expertly into her cupped hand. 'As I said, it's nothing really. I'll go next month. The state of your schoolwork is *much* more important, don't you think?'

'Y-e-es,' said Charlotte slowly, but her brain was whirring. Something was going on. And she strongly suspected that it involved lobster thermidor and dark chocolate mousse.

*   *   *

Over the next few days, Charlotte's wheedling and coaxing got her absolutely nowhere. Polite comments about book groups elicited polite replies from her mother—and nothing more. Yes, she'd managed to rearrange the book group for another night. Yes, it was perfectly reasonable to be a member of four book groups. She'd quit the lowbrow one the week before, as a matter of fact—something to do with a gold-trimmed Trollope—so it was only three now. And no, she didn't expect that they'd be reading *Jane Eyre*.

But just when she'd almost given up, a tentative suggestion that Charlotte herself should go along to see what all the fuss was about was greeted with enthusiasm.

'What a marvellous idea,' Mrs Penman said. 'We'll be discussing Tolstoy's *War and Peace* next. Read it in time for next month's book group and you can come along.' She delved into her enormous handbag and wrestled a brick of a book from it, placing the weighty tome carefully—neither bending pages nor breaking the spine—in front of her dumbstruck daughter. 'We'd love to hear your opinions.'

Oh.

Charlotte looked at the book. Then at her mum. Then back at the book.

Disappointingly, but unsurprisingly, it hadn't shrunk. 'What's it about?' she asked, her voice squeaking higher as she forced the words out. The gigantic proportions of the novel told her that this was no light read.

A smile connoisseur might have described Mrs Penman's grin as a delicate blend of gleeful and smug, with a hefty dollop of don't-try-to-outwit-me-matey.

'War,' she said. 'And peace.'

'Ah . . .' said Charlotte, nodding. 'So the clue's in the title.'

'You've got it,' said Mum. 'Plenty of brooding heroes, but no one to rival your Mr Rochester.' Her expression softened as she smoothed a stray curl from her daughter's brow. 'Now, my dear, I suggest that you stop being so nosey and concentrate on getting into my good books, instead of my book group. A spot of homework would do nicely. Imagine how wonderful it would be for me to boast about the effort you're putting in at the parents' evening . . .'

All of which meant that Charlotte

was no further on in her quest to discover the deep, dark secret that she was sure nestled inside this 'book group'. Because, if anything was going on, Mrs Penman wasn't telling.

Deeply unsatisfied with the lack of results from her investigation and beginning to wonder if she'd imagined her mother's blushes in the first place, Charlotte retired to her room. She paused to admire the small, but beautifully formed button nose of the bass guitarist who was occupying her coveted number-one spot this week and whose poster was stuck to her bedroom door. Then she fired off a speedy email to Dad, who was in Singapore this week, struggling with the difficulties thrown up by revolutionary new disc brakes. Then, raking exploratory furrows through the mess of her desk, her fingers closed around the one thing that she knew would take her mind off things. Hugging *Jane Eyre* tightly to her, she wriggled onto the windowsill.

Within minutes, all thoughts of make-believe book clubs, French teachers and homework had drifted away like ragged mist warmed by the sun over Thornfield.

CHAPTER EIGHT

Until now, Charlotte had been totally convinced that the most terrible sound in the world was an unsupervised school orchestra of caterwauling recorders and clarinets. But this was enough to make your ears bleed.

It had been Miss Stone's bright idea that pupils should attend parents' evening. Apparently, this would add a new dimension to the proceedings. Bad move. From the frantic arching of her eyebrows and the flapping of her hands, it appeared that the head teacher had realised her mistake—but too late to do anything about the furious arguments in progress.

Tables were placed around the edge of the hall, a teacher barricaded behind each, back firmly to the wall. Before each was a once-orderly queue of seats, already jerked out of position by impatient parents and their reluctant offspring.

Charlotte took a few minutes to absorb the atmosphere and, as her ears slowly became used to the noise, distinct sounds began to rise above the thunderous roar: teachers complaining to parents about their children's schoolwork; parents berating children for their lack of effort; children protesting that teachers were being totally unfair and that they'd been working hard, no really, they *had*; and teachers disputing that they'd been unfair and were just trying to teach badly behaved pupils basic facts.

It was chaotic. It was shambolic. It was *brilliant*.

Across the crowded hall, Charlotte spotted her mother, who was bobbing her head up and down like a nodding dog as she listened attentively to one eager parent. Mrs Penman glanced in her daughter's direction and looked pointedly at her watch. Charlotte did the same. There were only five minutes to go before it was her turn to be paraded around the hall like a prize Chihuahua.

Just two tables away from her mother, Mr Grant was suffering the onslaught of a parental double dose. They stabbed the air repeatedly with accusing fingers, pausing only to stroke their child's head, while she smiled sweetly at everyone. Mr Grant pursed his lips, looking for all the world as if he were sucking a wasp.

From this safe distance, Charlotte had the perfect opportunity to ponder the French teacher without risk of either a quick-fire question or a sarcastic comment. He was glowering for England. Quite possibly Scotland, Wales and Ireland too. *And* France. Hmmm. The man really was a worthy successor to mean and moody Mr Rochester. The question was: would her mother be able to see through the grumpiness to the charming man Charlotte was sure lay beneath? Unless she already had . . . That couldn't be ruled out.

Suddenly, Mr Grant's pupil burst into tears and was hurried away by her doting parents. The teacher looked up and scowled randomly around the assembly hall. 'Next!' he mouthed, his voice swallowed by the hideous racket.

'Yoohoo!' said a voice close enough to be heard. 'Are you ready?' Mrs Penman smiled enquiringly.

'Oh yes,' Charlotte replied, as Miss Stone hurried past with a box of Kleenex. 'Who's first?'

*   *   *

The maths teacher was quietly pleased with Charlotte's progress, going so far as to smile at her success with quadratic equations.

The English teacher complimented Charlotte on her expert use of apostrophes, clearly not realising that she'd been practising them since she could wield a crayon and, in their household, to misplace one of the curly blighters was akin to getting the name of the Prime Minister wrong.

The science teacher looked at her and scratched his grey head before announcing confidently, 'Marvellous.

67

Simply marvellous. Keep up the good work, Andrea.'

Before commenting, the PE teacher rubbed her hands thoughtfully on the tennis skirt that she wore over her tracksuit bottoms. Apart from uncharacteristic success at the long jump, which was quite obviously due to long legs rather than athletic ability, she didn't see why Charlotte bothered turning up for PE at all. Privately, Charlotte didn't see why the PE teacher turned up either when all she did was blow-dry her hair while the pupils hung around the gym like fruit bats. Publicly, she treated the teacher to her most insincere smile.

Neither of them was quite sure what the geography teacher had said, as there was a fight taking place at the adjoining desk.

And then it was time for French.

Mr Grant looked up warily as they approached.

'Ah, Charlotte,' he said. 'And her delightful mother. How nice.'

It was just the sort of comment Charlotte was used to the teacher drawling in class, his words dripping with sarcasm. They were off to a good start then. Now all she needed was for her mother to join in the irony-fest and she could wave goodbye to that bridesmaid's dress for ever. Briefly, Charlotte wondered if she was doing the right thing. Did she really want years of brooding moodiness at the breakfast table from this man? Then she reminded herself sternly that it was Mum she should be thinking of. And while Mr Rochester couldn't be described as a bundle of laughs, he was a top bloke deep down. Very deep down. So, deep inside Mr Grant there was probably a stand-up comic trying to get out. Probably. Hastily, she dragged her attention back to the approaching battle. Had she missed anything?

'Mr Grant,' Mrs Penman was saying, her expression stony. She didn't appear to be putting it on. That put paid to the secret-evenings-out-in-lieu-of-the-book-group theory. 'Enjoying the evening, are you?'

'Marvellous,' he said.

'Excellent,' she replied.

Charlotte coughed politely to remind them she was there.

'Now, we can do this one of two ways,' said Mr Grant, plucking absent-mindedly at his cuff links, before turning a withering gaze on Mrs Penman. 'Option one is that you kick off with a tongue lashing, demand to know why Charlotte isn't quoting large sections of *A La Recherche Du Temps Perdu* over breakfast and finish with a dissection of my supposedly substandard teaching ability.' He paused and looked suddenly weary. 'Or you might like to go with option two, where I can tell you that *when* your daughter pays attention, she shows a promising aptitude for French. Which is it to be?'

Was this an imposter? Were they sitting at the wrong table? Charlotte barely had time to close her slack jaw before her mother spoke.

'Option two would be just perfect,' said Mrs Penman, with not a drop of irony. 'Promising, you say?'

Clunk! Charlotte's jaw clunked open

again. They were *both* acting like adults! This was spooky.

'Oh yes,' said Mr Grant, whose voice had dropped to a reasonable level now the furious crowds were thinning out and the noise was abating. 'With a little effort, I'm sure Charlotte will be doing her bit for the United Nations in due course.'

Charlotte sniffed the air for alcohol fumes, but there wasn't a whiff. She smiled doubtfully. This was uncharted territory. Mr Grant was being pleasant? Her mum wasn't arguing with him? Was that the chiming of church bells she could hear in the distance?

Ding dong!

Mrs Penman flushed. 'I . . . er . . . I–I should probably . . . er . . . take . . .'

Take you out for a drink? Take you for a ride in my car? Take you on a minibreak to Paris and learn French myself? Myriad possibilities pinged around Charlotte's romance-addled brain.

'. . . take this opportunity to apologise for my . . . er . . . comments

71

about your . . . um . . . teaching,' said Mrs Penman in an undertone. 'It was thoughtless of me, not to mention a little . . . er . . . rude.'

It was the French teacher's turn to look stunned—and Charlotte's turn to feel amazed. 'That's . . . er . . . jolly sporting of you,' he replied. 'It's entirely possible that I overreacted. A tough morning with the Year 7s, I seem to remember.' He twisted his mouth into something approximating a smile.

Mum's laughter tinkled like a garden water feature.

There was a fine line between blah-blah-blah and bleurgh and Charlotte had the uncomfortable feeling that the two teachers were about to cross it. No way did she want to witness *that*. Now, if she were to slide ever so c-a-r-e-f-u-l-l-y from her seat and creep ever so s-l-o-w-l-y away from this charming tête-à-tête, neither one would notice she'd gone and they'd be sipping Merlot by sundown. Experimentally, she shifted a millimetre to the right.

'Going somewhere?' asked her mother.

'Home?' suggested Charlotte optimistically.

'Then wouldn't it be sensible to wait for me? We both live there.'

'Ah, well,' began Charlotte, gliding seamlessly into her master-match-maker role. 'You've got more to discuss, I've got homework . . . It makes perfect sense that I let you continue your very important discussion with Mr Grant.' She ducked to collect her bag. ' 'Bye!'

'Nice try,' said Mrs Penman before turning back to the French teacher. 'Well, Mr Grant . . .'

'Oh, I don't think we need to be so formal,' he said, straightening his tie. 'Linda, isn't it?'

There was that tinkling laugh again. Pointedly, Charlotte turned away . . . and found herself staring right into the avocado eyes of the boy sitting on the next table. Jack Burley.

Wow.

He stared back.

Charlotte's stomach did a curious and not entirely unpleasant flip as she wondered where the rest of the room had gone.

And then he winked.

Had someone turned the heating up? Charlotte's cheeks were burning. She didn't need a mirror to tell her that she was pinker than a rare steak. Quick, she should seize the moment! Where was that Hollywood smile she'd perfected? How did it go? Wide and dazzling with a playful tilt of the head? That was it. Ready, steady . . . *showtime*!

Too late.

Jack Burley had turned away. He was lost to her, embroiled in a discussion about the finer points of on-time homework delivery.

Silvery objects flashed and jangled in Charlotte's line of vision.

'Huh?' she said stupidly, focusing at last on the dancing car keys. 'Oh. Right.'

Time to go.

Typical. For the first time this evening, she really wanted to stay.

CHAPTER NINE

A chaffinch or maybe a sparrow—given Charlotte's knowledge of nature, it could even have been a bald-headed eagle—hopped merrily along a branch and soared into a clear autumn sky that was interrupted only by small, fluffy clouds. She paused beside the front gate and breathed deeply. Ah . . . *L'air du car fumes*. Had there ever been a morning as marvellous as this?

'Your skirt's tucked in your knickers,' said Manda.

Charlotte spun round to look. 'W-w-what?'

'Gotcha.' Her friend gave a short, humourless laugh. 'How come you look so pleased with yourself?' She didn't wait for an answer. 'I got a right rollocking last night. According to Dad, maths is more important than life itself. Like I *really* need to know how long it takes seven and a half men to dig a hole two by two by four metres if each shovel holds 37mm^3 of soil and they dig at a rate of twelve shovelfuls a minute and stop for a tea break every half hour and—'

'Half a man?' queried Charlotte.

'Well, a short one,' Manda said crossly. 'Or one that's incapable of showing affection. A Tory. Whatever.'

'It'd teach you to get plenty of tea bags in,' Charlotte said.

'Hmph,' snorted Manda. 'Come on. We'll be late. I don't want to add unpunctuality to my list of misdemeanours . . . and will you *stop* smiling!'

Charlotte ignored her. She couldn't have looked miserable if someone had ripped the cover of her prized 1983 Penguin edition of *Jane Eyre*. Well, maybe then. But every time she tried to pull her lips straight, they immediately sprang back into a stupidly cheesy grin. 'How did you get on with everyone else?' she asked. 'I bet the art teacher was gushing over your work. Go on, she was, wasn't she?'

'Might have been,' Manda said grudgingly.

'And science?'

'Yeah, OK.'

'English lit. ?'

'Mmm.'

'History?'

Manda lifted up her hands in surrender. 'So I'm a genius who can't add up. Now tell me why you're so disgustingly happy or I'll punch you.'

'He winked,' Charlotte said. 'Jack Burley winked at me.'

'He never!' spluttered Manda. 'Really? Are you sure he didn't have something in his eye? It wasn't a tick?'

'He winked,' repeated Charlotte. Goodness, this must be how brides felt—and bridesmaids for that matter. Her face was actually starting to *ache*. 'Jack winked,' she said again, for good measure. Ooh, that felt *good*.

'Whoa . . .' said Manda. 'And then what?'

'Well, er . . .'

Manda leaned forward expectantly, like a tortoise peering out of its shell. 'Yes?'

'That was it,' admitted Charlotte in a small voice. She felt suddenly sad, and realised that her face muscles were no longer hurting. The smile must have gone. 'But it was a *lovely* wink,' she added wistfully.

She was immediately swamped by doubts. Had the boy of her dreams—as she'd belatedly realised he was—had something in his eye after all? Had he been looking at someone else? She didn't know. But whatever he'd been doing, she wanted more than anything for him to do it again. 'There *was* something else, actually.' Charlotte stuffed her hands in her jacket pockets, grimacing as her fingers encountered something sticky.

'Uh-huh?'

'My mum and Mr Grant hit it off.' She watched Manda's face contort through a series of comedy expressions, counting while the news sunk in. One . . . two . . . thr—

'What?!'

'Yep.' Smug didn't begin to describe how Charlotte felt. This was only the start. She might extend her matchmaking skills to the school yard next—after she'd secured Jack Burley's affections, of course. One had to have priorities.

'How?' asked Manda, eyes agog. 'I thought they didn't even *like* each other.'

Charlotte shrugged, feeling a warm glow of contentment. Or perhaps indigestion. She'd eaten breakfast *very* quickly. 'They do now.'

'So what did you *do*?' said Manda.

Charlotte considered the question carefully. 'I facilitated their meeting,' she announced at last.

'Have you been watching too much American telly?' asked Manda, her eyebrows wriggling like worms. 'Speak English, for Pete's sake.'

'They met at the parents' meeting,' Charlotte admitted. 'So it wouldn't have happened if it hadn't been for me. They'd have been talking to other parents rather than each other.' An enjoyable daydream invaded her thoughts, in which Mr Grant was toasting her good self and Jack was applauding wildly. 'I expect they'll thank me during the wedding speeches. I hope they aren't too embarrassing.'

'To recap,' said Manda, 'you didn't

actually *do* anything. Sometimes, Charlotte, you are so full of—' She broke off mid-rant and neatly sidestepped a small pile of dog mess. 'I'd be surprised if *anything* actually happened. I bet they're still at loggerheads and you're too fixated with Jane Eyre and Mr Rochester to separate fact from fiction.'

Charlotte drew herself up to her full height. 'I am not full of—' She negotiated another pavement sculpture. What was with dogs today? Had they dined on All Bran? 'They made an arrangement to discuss my school work further.' She tapped Manda on the shoulder to make sure she was paying attention. 'Over coffee. I'd say they're pretty much an item.'

They arrived at school as the last echoes of the school bell faded. Manda turned to face her. They were officially late. 'Is that so?' she asked.

'That's so,' said Charlotte firmly.

'Just to clarify,' said Manda, 'that's our very own Mr Grant, the French teacher with the humour deficit . . .'

Charlotte nodded.

'. . . and Mrs Penman, your very own mum.'

She nodded again.

'Then, if the French teacher and the English lit. teacher are an item,' recapped Manda with infuriating repetitiveness, 'why has the French teacher just arrived at school in the company of a woman that is neither a teacher nor your mother?' She looked pointedly over Charlotte's shoulder—arms folded, lips squished into an uncompromising line. Self-satisfaction was scrawled across her expression.

Her heart plummeting faster than the FTSE 100 after a run on the bank, Charlotte swung round to see her future stepfather clambering out of an orange Lotus Elise. (She knew this not because she was a *Top Gear* fan, but because it was written on the car.) His pinstripe suit looked remarkably like the one he'd worn to yesterday's parents' evening, only more crumpled. Mr Grant quickly fastened the top button of his shirt and tightened his tie.

Charlotte would have liked to strangle him with it.

Then, to make matters so much worse, the French teacher leaned over the door of the low-slung sports car and *kissed* the gorgeous woman in the driver's seat. On both cheeks. She smiled, waved gaily and sped away. The car engine's throaty roar was mocking as it departed.

'Well, isn't that just marvellous,' said Charlotte. 'Blanche Ingram has arrived.'

CHAPTER TEN

'*How* do you know her name?' gasped Manda.

Charlotte pounded on down the corridor, her reply punctuated by sharp intakes of breath. 'Everyone . . . knows . . . her . . . name,' she puffed. 'She's . . . his . . . fancy . . . woman.'

'You what?' asked Manda incredulously. 'And you tried to fix your *mum* up with him, knowing that he was taken?' She looked horrified.

Charlotte skidded to a halt outside

the salmon-pink classroom door and peered through the wire mesh of the reinforced glass window.

A sea of heads faced Mrs Hook. The teacher was jabbing an accusing finger at the assembled class like a frenzied woodpecker. Then she looked up and caught sight of the two latecomers. Her finger did an about-turn and curled to beckon them inside.

*   *   *

One serious and highly embarrassing ticking off later, they were slouching in the back row of the assembly hall. Charlotte was studying her favourite Isle-of-Wight-shaped crack in the ceiling with grim intent. Manda sat stony-faced in the next seat, a pink spot of crossness burning high on each cheek.

Miss Stone had chosen to open the assembly with the baffling morality tale of a farmer sowing seed. Some seed fell on fertile ground and grew like billyo, while some seed fell on weedy ground and was choked by weeds, while still

more—there was an awful lot of seed—
fell on stony ground and failed to
sprout. This led Charlotte to conclude
that if the farmer was daft enough to
throw his seed onto weedy and stony
ground, then he should probably be
doing a different job.

She scanned the platform, her eyes
coming to a halt on Mr Grant. The
Love Rat, as he now was. He sat on an
orange plastic chair, one leg casually
flung over the other, his expression
blank. So he thought he could keep her
poor, devoted mother dangling while
he zipped around in fast cars with
Blanche, did he? Was he trying to make
her jealous? Or, horror of horrors, was
he—here she faltered, hardly able to
contemplate the possibility—going to
see them both *at the same time*?

Noooooooooo!

She couldn't let this happen. The
Love Rat couldn't be allowed to cavort
around blamelessly seducing woman-
kind, sowing his wild oats . . .
'Arrrgggghhh!' she screamed silently,
cursing the unwanted reappearance of
the farming metaphor.

All around her, pupils started to fidget, signalling that assembly was nearly over. There was just Miss Stone's parting salvo to endure.

'I have just *two* notices this morning!' she bellowed.

Her unwilling audience winced at the sound and the prospect.

'Firstly, I'd like to congratulate David Trousdale . . .' The head teacher paused and jerked her head at a small, earnest-looking boy wearing unfortunate-looking glasses—had round tortoiseshell frames ever suited anyone? He stared back uncomprehendingly. Miss Stone raised her eyebrows. David raised his. In despair, she extended her right arm and pointed imperiously at her victim as if her finger was a magic wand in disguise. 'You, boy! On your feet!'

Realising at last that he was to be made a public spectacle of, David struggled upright to await his fate. It wasn't long in coming.

'You've been keeping a secret from us, haven't you, Mr Trousdale?' continued Miss Stone. Her thin lips parted to reveal teeth in dire need of celebrity bleaching. She smiled fiendishly.

There were uncomfortable sniggers from pupils relieved not to be in David's shoes. Which was just about everyone else.

'Something you do in your room at night?' the head teacher added.

This was just too much. Uncontrollable laughter roared around the hall as David bunched his shoulders and tried, unsuccessfully, to bury his head in his neck.

Now it was Miss Stone's turn to look confused. But with a shrug, she carried on. 'I am delighted to announce that David Trousdale has been awarded a Blue Peter badge for his magnificent model of the London Eye, made entirely from recycled earplugs. Isn't that right, David?'

There was an answering mumble that could quite easily have been a 'yes' or a groan of despair. David sank back onto his seat and jabbed his chortling neighbour in the ribs.

'Super!' boomed Miss Stone

enthusiastically. She squinted at her notes. 'Secondly and finally . . .' The head teacher rearranged her face into a wide smile.

'Uh-oh,' whispered Manda. 'She's going to be funny.'

'I'm sure you'll all join me in thanking the teachers for their invaluable help and support at yesterday's parents' evening.' The head teacher gave a small, satisfied nod. Here it came . . . 'They certainly *taught* us a thing or two about the importance of communication. It was a *lesson* in getting along.' Miss Stone looked intensely pleased with herself.

There was an uncomprehending silence.

The head teacher's beatific smile faded as she skimmed the rows of dumb pupils and her face resumed its usual glare. 'Right,' she said briskly, as her comic career failed to take off once more. 'Back to your classrooms!'

As they streamed out of the hall, Charlotte looked back. Her eyes locked with Mr Grant's. He was staring right at her, his expression dark and unreadable. Fuelled by repulsion at his two-timing, she scowled back.

There was no response. Not a flicker.

Deflated, she turned to leave.

'Hey, you're in a hurry!' said Mrs Penman, gripping her daughter by the shoulders to halt her flight. 'Going somewhere important?'

Charlotte felt her lips move, but had no idea what she said. Her mind was busily occupied elsewhere. It was up on the stage, to be precise, re-examining the exact angle of Mr Grant's look. The Love Rat hadn't been staring at *her*—of course he hadn't.

He'd been staring at her mother.

*   *   *

Never had Charlotte been quite so pleased to see the dining hall. The morning's lessons had lasted *for ever*. Physics was mind-boggling. And a momentary lapse of memory—she'd forgotten her trainers, again—had resulted in a riveting hour and ten minutes spent restuffing saggy beanbags.

After handing over borrowed cash—she'd forgotten her dinner money too—at the till, she surveyed the packed hall. There was no chance of finding a quiet corner in here. Or Jack Burley, for a long-overdue gaze. It was swarming with pupils. Rain was streaming down the windows, condensation obscuring the wild autumn day outside. There was hardly a seat to spare.

'Over here!'

Manda was perched on the end of a table crammed with boys. She waved at Charlotte, who wove her way between the tables towards her, relieved that her friend's earlier anger had now dissolved into minor irritation, directed mainly against the teaching establishment's petty rules about punctuality.

'I don't think I've seen it this busy since they sold chips,' Charlotte said.

'Yeah, right,' said Manda, who clearly had other things on her mind. She speared a parcel of ravioli. 'Don't you think it's about time you explained?'

'Huh?' said Charlotte.

'Blanche Ingram.'

'Oh . . .' Charlotte couldn't help laughing, hurriedly biting her lip when she saw Manda's warning look. She suddenly realised how her comments about fancy women could have been misconstrued, especially if she hadn't made it clear she was talking about Mr Rochester. 'She's the woman that hangs around Thornfield trying to nab herself a trophy husband. You know, the loaded one,' she said.

Her best friend stared as blankly as if Charlotte had accidentally slipped into Serbo-Croat.

'Blanche Ingram is a character in *Jane Eyre*,' said Charlotte guiltily.

Manda chewed slowly, swallowing her pasta and digesting the news. 'So, that woman this morning—you don't actually know her at all?'

'Er . . . no,' admitted Charlotte. 'But look at the evidence. She dropped him off at school wearing last night's clothes. He kissed her. Twice. She drives a sports car. She's *got* to be trouble.'

Her best friend smiled for the first time since registration. 'Then we have to find out who she *is*, don't we?' she said. She popped another piece of ravioli into her mouth and munched thoughtfully, dabbing her mouth with a napkin before continuing. 'But first, we have to get one thing straight. Repeat after me: Mr Grant is *not* Mr Rochester, my mum is *not* Jane Eyre and we are *not* living in the nineteenth century.'

'Spoilsport,' said Charlotte. She smiled and began to eat her lunch.

CHAPTER ELEVEN

Of course, it wasn't as simple as all that. Without access to police records or, at the very least, a tracking device attached to the underside of the orange Lotus, they had no chance of finding Blanche Ingram. (Manda had grudgingly agreed to call her this in the absence of any evidence to the contrary. As Charlotte pointed out, they didn't know that she *wasn't* called Blanche Ingram. And it *was* a pretty cool name.) They didn't even have a library card or a discarded cinema ticket stub to track her down.

It was all becoming horribly familiar. Charlotte realised that so far, any progress in her Grand Plan had been achieved by good, old-fashioned luck. However much she tried to skew the facts, it had nothing to do with her excellent—but admittedly untested and unproven—detective skills.

'Excuse meeeeeee!' A skater looped past her at speed, stroking his wheels on the frosty Tarmac in a Michael-Jackson-style moonwalk. His face—travelling backwards, as indeed, he was—was a mixture of terror and exhilaration.

Charlotte grinned, then winced as the skater narrowly missed a doddery pensioner. There was a distant *ooops* as he cannoned into a bench further along the seafront and dangled over it in a Lycra-clad tangle of purple limbs. Seconds later, he was off again, dodging the assorted wanderers, strollers and joggers crowding the promenade.

It was a stunning afternoon. The sun, sunk so low that it seemed in perilous danger of plopping into the sea, glowed red. But there was no warmth in it, thankfully. Charlotte was wearing enough fleece to clothe a flock of sheep. Any more warmth and she might bleat. Or spontaneously combust. Mrs Penman was convinced that there was no such thing as being too warm during the winter, unless you happened to be inside, in which case all outer clothing must be shed until shivering point was reached. This was in order to *feel the benefit* of the many layers of fabric that were piled on before stepping into the cold outdoors again. The logic was baffling. But it was not an argument Charlotte considered to be high on her list of Things Worth Fighting For, so she continued to boil and shiver and, in the process, kept Mum happy.

Charlotte spied an empty bench and hurried towards it. She sat down and stared out to sea. Waves rolled in and out, in . . . and out. Seen through the wrought-iron curlicues of the beach railings, the tiny segments of seascape were oddly disconnected, like the different pieces of her Grand Plan.

This was the moment where a ghostly voice, echoing mysteriously across the sea, would come in *really* handy. *'Charlotte . . . Charlotte . . .'* it would wail, and then provide a few clues to Blanche Ingram's identity and a few choice matchmaking tips.

Charlotte strained her ears hopefully, but was not altogether surprised that the ghostly voice refused to oblige. That sort of thing only happened in books.

She decided to make a list instead. They always made her feel in control.

Scrabbling in her pockets for writing materials, she eventually found a pencil that she'd squirrelled away in case of an emergency celebrity-autograph opportunity. Her coat yielded a flyer for a club she was way too young for, but she'd kept because she was so totally thrilled to have been given it in the first place—apparently, being lanky did have *some* advantages other than being able to spot bald patches belonging to short men. In the absence of a narrow-feint ring-bound notebook, this would have to do. She flipped it over and began to write.

> ***Objective One:*** Find Mum suitable Mr Rochester for marriage purposes.
> *Progress:* Partial success. Possibly. Looking good, anyway. Sort of.
> *Action:* Let true love take its course (helping in case of <u>dire</u> emergency).

> ***Objective Two:*** Discover true identity of Blanche Ingram/ orange-Lotus-driving-scarlet-woman/Mr Grant's 'bit on the side' in order to eliminate from potential love triangle with Mum <u>by any means necessary</u>.
> *Progress:* Chuff all.
> *Action:* Goodness knows.

And then, because she was feeling a

little reckless after the winking incident
. . .

Objective Three: Convince Jack
   Burley that I'm not a total fool.
Progress: Zero.
Action: Personality transplant?

Charlotte sucked her pencil, then spat in disgust. *Urgh.* Worse than Brussels sprouts.

She surveyed her notes with a critical eye. Not as dismal as they might have been, but not as good as she'd hoped. What she needed was something to help her with her enquiries. A jaw-dropping revelation would be nice—that or a private detective on a *very* low hourly rate.

Fondly, she allowed her mind to wander back to Mr Rochester's dramatic declaration in *Jane Eyre*. *So* cool. *So* romantic . . . Now, if Mr Grant would play ball by announcing equally honourable intentions towards her mother, then she'd be well on the way to complete success. He was obviously totally in love with Mum. Cappuccino silk rippled enticingly in her mind's eye followed by a tantalising glimpse of moss-green eyes. (She couldn't seem to help Jack Burley popping up in her thoughts nowadays. It was very disconcerting, but not at all unpleasant.)

Cwoark!

A squawking seagull awoke Charlotte from her daydream. She looked curiously at the huge bird, which was standing regally on the concrete groyne that stretched out to sea. And that's when it came to her. One blinding flash of insight later, she knew what she had to do.

It was obvious, really.

She had to speak to Mum.

It was time to come clean. Not totally clean, obviously. Charlotte had now decided that Mr Grant's imminent marriage proposal to her mother was as inevitable as sunset, sunrise and the fact that an accidentally dropped bag of shopping *will* contain eggs. But if Mum knew it was coming, she would freak out and ruin all of Charlotte's carefully laid wedding plans. And then

Blanche Ingram would have won and she'd whisk the French teacher away to an unbearably perfect life of luxury and expensive orange cars.

So, telling the whole truth and nothing but would be madness. But perhaps a little gentle quizzing and a few well-placed hints would prepare Mum for a lifetime of wedded bliss. And once she'd waved them off on the honeymoon, Charlotte could ponder those mossy eyes at her leisure.

Charlotte clasped her hands together in what she imagined was a pretty authentic nineteenth-century style. There was no time like the present. She jumped to her feet, turned her back on the glittering sea and walked purposefully away. The beach huts were psychedelic in the autumn sunshine.

Indigestion-remedy pink . . .

Egg-yolk yellow . . .

Vomit green.

Oh. That wasn't paint.

Ick.

She sidled between two huts and crossed the large green, heading for home. The calming swoosh of the sea was soon drowned out by roaring traffic.

CHAPTER TWELVE

It felt good to have made a decision. It was just a shame that Charlotte's stomach hadn't registered this fact. As she unhooked the gate, it fizzed and gurgled like a mad scientist's experiment. On the third fumbled attempt, she poked her key into the lock and turned it.

She was home.

Mum wasn't.

Talk about anti-climax. Charlotte sank onto the bottom stair with a loud *ooof* of disappointment, and a spot of relief. It wasn't too late to back out. She only had to explain to *herself* that she'd bottled it. No one else would ever know.

'Hellooooo!'

Too late.

'Why are you sitting there, pet?' said

Mrs Penman, breezing into the hallway with a pair of hessian shopping bags and a telltale brown paper bag. 'Too weak to climb the stairs? You can't be eating enough vegetables. How many portions have you had today?'

'One,' replied Charlotte, without even having to think. She answered this question on a regular basis. 'Grapefruit juice. What's in the bag?'

Mum smiled mysteriously. 'I just happened to drop into my favourite shop,' she said. 'Here, it's for you.' The bag's crinkled surface bore a picture of a teetering pile of paperbacks underneath the moniker *Barnham's Books*.

This was *so* not the time to be given surprise presents, not when she had such a delicate topic to broach. Charlotte bared her teeth in a rough approximation of a smile. She was so fired up for matchmaking that she wanted to get on with it. Right now. Although . . . her breathing slowed and became shallower as she pulled the book from its 100 per cent recyclable wrapping (it said so on the bag).

'Oooooh . . .' If there was one thing that could distract her, it was this.

'Do you like it?' said Mum. 'I didn't think you had this one—and it was on special offer.'

'Lovely . . .' breathed Charlotte. She ran her fingers over the familiar features—the heavy brow, the short nose, the firm chin and the serene, knowing expression. No one could ever accuse her favourite author of being a looker. She read the title aloud. *'Charlotte Brontë: A Passionate Life.* Are you sure?'

'Oh, yes,' said Mum. 'I'd take "passionate" with a handful of salt though—there isn't too much bodice-ripping going on between the covers. At least, I didn't spot any when I flicked through it.' She bent down to pick up the shopping. 'I've being hearing marvellous things from Mr Grant about your good behaviour at school,' she said, by way of explanation. 'I thought you deserved a treat—one that won't rot your teeth.'

'Ah, yes,' said Charlotte. This was it—her big chance.

'Mmm?' said Mum.

'Well, the thing is . . .' began Charlotte. She fanned the pages of the Brontë biography with her thumb. Crikey, this was difficult. She tried again. 'I was wondering if you might like to . . . er . . . well, er . . . get yourself a, well . . .'

Mrs Penman looked expectant.

For a few moments, the only sound was the soft blip-blopping of the radiator.

'Ithoughtyoumightlikeaboyfriend!' gabbled Charlotte.

Her mum giggled. She replaced the shopping bags on the hall carpet, threw back her head and . . .

. . . and laughed!

Apparently, Charlotte was really funny.

'Ha ha!' she laughed. 'Ha ha, ha ha!'

Charlotte got the message.

'*HA HA HA—*'

Now she was overdoing it.

'When would I, er . . . well, how do I have time for a man, boy, um . . . boyfriend?'

Was it Charlotte or was her mum

acting guiltily? In an earlier, calmer moment, Charlotte had identified two likely scenarios following her super-subtle question. They were (in order of preference):

1. Mum agrees that she needs a gorgeous guy with sideburns and we proceed with all due care and attention to the local bride frock shop.
2. Mum tells me to butt out.

She certainly hadn't contemplated:

3. Mum laughs like a drain.

'Why would I need a man when I've got such a marvellous daughter?' Mum said, when she'd stopped giggling and snorting.

'I'll put the kettle on,' said Charlotte, getting up and making her way to the kitchen. Mentally, she added tabloid journalist and hard-nosed political interviewer to the pile of Jobs She'd Be No Good At. But her annoyance at her mum's reaction receded in the face of such a compliment.

'It won't fit,' spluttered Mrs Penman, losing it once more.

Charlotte sighed. Shopping bags weren't the only things that were recycled in this house. She concentrated on making the drinks until Mum decided to act her age, swirling in enough milk to achieve just the right shade of beige—darker than milk chocolate, lighter than the living-room carpet. (Her mother was very fussy.)

Daaa ding diddle-ing, diddle-ing ding DING ding . . .

The theme from *The Sound of Music* jangled around the kitchen in all its polyphonic glory. Frantically, Mrs Penman plunged both hands into her handbag and began rooting about for her mobile as if it were a time bomb in need of defusing. As she pressed a key to answer it, she mouthed 'sorry' to her daughter.

Saved by the ringtone, for now. But not for long—Charlotte would make sure of that. A little gentle interrogation and a lot of patience was all that was needed. She quivered with excitement as her mum listened intently to the caller's words. She was *so* close to wearing that bridesmaid's dress—by now, redesigned as a stylish ivory number with a cappuccino sash—that she could almost feel the cool silk slipping between her fingers.

'You're kidding,' said Mum. All laughter ceased as the colour drained from her face.

Charlotte's attention snapped back to the telephone conversation. There was News.

'No . . .' said Mum, her eyes wide with horror. 'Seriously?'

Bad News.

'*Next week?*' shrieked Mum.

Very Bad News.

Mrs Penman carefully laid the phone down next to her perfectly beige coffee. 'I think I'll have a splash of brandy in that,' she quavered. 'I knew it might happen, but it's always a shock when it does, isn't it? And it's such short notice . . . How *will* I be ready for Monday?'

By now, she sounded more like a

dentist's drill than an English teacher and Charlotte grew more concerned by the wail. 'What *is* it?' she asked.

'The Ofsted inspectors are coming,' said Mum.

CHAPTER THIRTEEN

Ofsted changed everything.

In seconds, Mrs Penman morphed from a mother on the brink of a new romantic attachment (with added sideburns) into a teacher on the verge of losing the plot. Despite Charlotte's entreaties to get back to the topic in hand, she wouldn't. *Couldn't*. Her vocabulary had wizened and shrunk like an old lady in dire need of wrinkle cream.

Charlotte emailed Dad—now in Japan—for advice on dealing with Mum. 'Run!' he replied, not altogether helpfully. 'Trust me, it won't be pretty.'

It wasn't.

'It was weird,' Charlotte told Manda later. 'One minute, she was right where

I wanted her . . . and the next, it was like she was plugged into the National Grid. The only words she could say were *lesson plans* and *omigod*. A lot. Goodness knows what time she went to bed, but her office was wrecked this morning. There were plastic wallets *everywhere*.' She lowered her voice. 'I found an empty wine bottle too. *And* she'd eaten the Green & Black's chocolate that I'd hidden at the back of the fridge.'

Manda gasped. 'Not your 34% cocoa solids milk chocolate?' she whispered.

Charlotte nodded regretfully.

She and Manda were unbelievably early, partly because they wanted to avoid another showdown and partly because a tight-lipped, slightly greenish-looking Mrs Penman had offered them a lift to school. As soon as they'd arrived, she'd shot off in the direction of the staff room, *without* going back to check that the car was locked. Not even once. The Ofsted inspectors must be Exceedingly Bad News to distract Mum from her obsessive-compulsive leanings.

'Blimey . . .' said Manda, staring in awe across the empty classroom.

'My *favourite* chocolate,' added Charlotte from her windowsill vantage point. It was the ideal spot to watch the slow trickle of pupils arriving in the school yard—and to check out the staff car park. There was no sign of the orange Lotus this morning. Mr Grant had skidded to a halt on his battered old bike—pinstripe suit trousers neatly tucked into antique metal bicycle clips. On his back was the mother of all rucksacks. On his face was an almighty scowl. After a cursory fiddle with his bike lock, the French teacher had hurried towards the staff room too. Charlotte couldn't help thinking that by now it must be rammed. A whole room of sweaty, panicky teachers, all banging on about lesson plans. Scary.

'So when are these wicked Ofstedders coming?'

Manda's voice was a squeakier than usual and Charlotte turned from the window to check she was OK.

'*Arrrggghhhhhh!*' she cried, staring in horror at the evil-looking contraption that Manda seemed to be inserting into her eye. 'What are you *doing*? Torturing yourself?'

'I am curling my eyelashes,' said Manda primly. 'It's quite safe. I saw someone doing this on the bus the other day—while it was *moving*.' She clamped her fist around the device and squeezed. 'Ouch. Got my eyelid there, I think.'

Charlotte winced. 'Why are you curling them anyway?' she asked curiously, making her way over to Manda's desk for a closer look. 'Are curly eyelashes in? Should I be doing it too?'

Manda readjusted the eyelash curlers and squeezed again. 'Ah . . . that's better.' She peered up at Charlotte, wearing an expression that was no doubt intended to be scornful, but when viewed through metal prongs ended up looking downright ridiculous.

Charlotte bit her lip and tried not to laugh.

'Actually, independent studies have shown that this makes eyelashes appear 36 per cent longer,' announced

Manda. 'If you add Super Lengthening Mascara With White Thickening Undercoat Combo, you can double that figure. And eyes seem 47 per cent wider too.' Carefully, she unclamped the device and jammed it onto her other eyelid. '*Ow.*'

'I'll tell you something else,' said Charlotte.

'What?'

'You look 100 per cent stupider.'

'Oh, ha ha.' Manda was annoyingly unperturbed. She pulled the curler free and batted her eyelashes. 'Want a go?'

Charlotte frowned thoughfully at the silvery gadget in Manda's outstretched hand. Why would she want to do something as daft as this? Everyone knew that boys respected a girl's inner self more than her outward appearance. They definitely weren't swayed by assets as superficial as a pair of pert wotsits and sticky-out eyelashes. Still, just in case . . . 'Go on then,' she said. 'Give it here.'

Jack Burley could have walked into the classroom when Charlotte's eyelashes had been boosted by 36 per cent. Even better, he could have walked in when they were lengthened and thickened to tarantula-leg proportions—although, if the independent studies were to be believed, she might have knocked him over with the gusts they created. He could have, but he didn't. Instead, he chose the moment when Charlotte was flailing around like a fish on a hook.

'Keep still!' ordered Manda, hanging onto the curlers for grim death. 'You're going to look *amazing*. Just like me. No one will be able to resist you!'

'They *will*,' moaned Charlotte, 'especially if I've got two black eyes. Let. Me. Go!'

'Ten seconds more.' Manda was calm, but surprisingly firm. 'Otherwise, you'll be totally lopsided and Jack will mistake you for that bloke in *Clockwork Orange*. He's not going to fancy you then, is he?'

Suddenly, and in excruciating slow motion, the classroom door was sucked shut by the huge hinge suspended above it. Which meant that the door had been open. Which meant that—

'Er . . . hi, Jack!' squeaked Manda.

Because it had to be him, didn't it? It couldn't have been some innocuous bystander who had no interest in watching a pair of girls wrestling each other. Oh no. It would have to be the one person that Charlotte *really* wanted to impress. Awkwardly, she disentangled herself from Manda's slackened grip and, with as much poise as she could muster—which wasn't a great deal—rubbed her eyes and straightened her school uniform. She swung round with a buoyant 'Hi!'

Jack was leaning against a desk at the front of the classroom, arms hugging his bulging rucksack. (What she wouldn't give to be that rucksack.) Charlotte examined him for blushes but his naturally glowing cheeks hid any clues. (*Darn* that gorgeous complexion.) Quickly she thought back, replaying the whole incriminating scene and trying to coordinate Manda's Jack-tastic outburst with the clang of the door shutting. What had he heard? Anything? Nothing? *Everything?*

'Hi,' he said. 'Do I need to separate

112

you pair—or were you having a group hug?' He raised an inquisitive eyebrow.

'No . . . er . . . ha ha! I mean, *yes*. That is . . . neither. Um . . .' Even Charlotte knew that she was acting as if aliens had stolen her brain. Goodness knows what Jack thought. She tried again. 'We were . . . er . . . we were . . .'

'We were talking about Ofsted,' said Manda calmly.

'Eh?' said Jack. He frowned. 'Are they a band?'

Yay! Silently thanking Manda for her quick thinking—and the aliens for returning her grey matter, Charlotte recited, 'It's the Office for Standards in Education.' She was safely back on firm ground thanks to Mum. 'They visit schools every couple of years to see if everything's up to scratch, make sure that teachers aren't filling our heads with rubbish, see if everyone knows how to spell *pterodactyl*, that sort of thing.'

'Oh, I see . . .' said Jack, who quite obviously didn't. Generously, Charlotte forgave him. A detailed knowledge of the Grim Reapers of Schooling, as her mother liked to call them, wasn't high on her list of must-have attributes anyway.

'They might shut the school down,' said Manda ominously.

'Really?' said Jack. *Now* he looked interested.

'Well . . . probably not,' said Charlotte, neatly lassoing his attention once again. 'They dish out plenty of warnings before they do that. But they give schools hardly any time to prepare, so don't expect any sense out of the teachers before the invasion.'

'No change there, then,' said Jack.

His grin was as irresistible as chocolate— Charlotte couldn't help but join in. Steadfastly ignoring the blush that was creeping across her face, she concentrated on committing Jack's eyes to memory. Now she was much closer she could see that they didn't remotely resemble pond water, wheatgrass, sprouts or avocado skin. They were more like . . . mould! That was it—the furry green mould that grows on bread if it's left long enough. With a start, she was suddenly aware of another startling fact: the mouldy eyes were staring back.

'Ahem.'

The spell was broken.

Charlotte turned to see her best friend languidly applying glittery pink lipgloss with a wand.

'Oh, sorry,' Manda said, unapologetically. 'Thought you'd both gone to sleep there.' She pressed her lips together and opened them with a sticky *mwah*. Boredom seeping from every pore, she glanced across at Jack. 'Look, if you want *Chas* to entertain you with more riveting stuff about Ofsted, then why don't you just swap email addresses. Eh?'

Charlotte froze. In the interminable pause that followed Manda's maddening suggestion, Jack found a sudden interest in his rucksack strap, while she pondered unpleasant ways to get her own back. (Tarring and feathering scored highly.) Eventually, she located her voice.

'Er . . . whatever! Very funny, Manda,' she said. 'Why would we want to do *that*?'

'Top idea,' said Jack. His rucksack buckle pinged open and he tugged a rough book from its murky depths. 'Here, bung your email in that.'

The world went all wibbly and dreamlike . . . *Her clumsy fingers took hold of the proffered book. Opened it. Eyes skimmed the page, the messy scribble, looking for a blank space. She felt a pen pushed into her hand. Wrote what she hoped was her email address, but could quite easily have been the recipe for pancake mixture.*

'Done?' said Jack. 'Cheers.' Head down, he stuffed the book in his rucksack and made for the back of the classroom at speed.

The bell for registration jangled.

And the world stopped being wibbly and dreamlike and turned twinkly instead.

Manda smiled like the cat who'd got the cream. And not just any old cream. This was heart-stoppingly delicious clotted cream churned from full-fat milk squeezed at midnight from Devon's finest cows by Devon's finest milkmaids. 'You can thank me over lunch tomorrow,' she purred.

CHAPTER FOURTEEN

That evening, Mum's manic mood swung like a pendulum between hysteria and pessimism. It grew increasingly difficult to work out which emotion was coming next, so Charlotte made a tactical withdrawal to her room, taking the laptop with her.

She hadn't been online for a couple of days, so there was a lot of catching up to do. The celebs had been out in force in Showbizland, going to buy milk in their (gasp!) jogging bottoms and doing unmentionable things with small dogs and handbags. It was a good half hour before she was reasonably up to speed.

Next, she checked her email. There were five messages in all—three from Manda, one from Catherine—her Canadian e-pal—and one from jackbee@hotmail.com. Great. *More* spam. She trailed her forefinger around the mouse pad, idly wondering what it would be this time. An evil virus that would erase the hard drive while simultaneously enrolling her on a pole-dancing master class in Soho.

There again, it might just be an email.

She clicked.

To: janeeyre2@gmail.com
From: jackbee@hotmail.com
Subject: A vitally important question

Q: What's the difference between bowls and boules?
A: Who cares? It's just a load of balls. Ha ha!
J

Oh. Right. Ha ha.

She paused—and a frisson of excitement sizzled through her body. She looked at the email address again. jackbee@hotmail.com. Eh? Could it be . . . ? No . . . Was this a trick? Or was it . . . an actual, true-life email from Ol' Green Eyes himself?

Oooh.

She examined the evidence.

'jackbee'—this *could* be Jack B, which *could* in turn be Jack Burley. Or Jacqueline Benson. Or Joaquin Beaulieu from Year 12. (Did his parents actively dislike him to brand the poor lad with such an unpronounceable name?)

Now, how about the Bad Joke? It might be their essay question for French this week, but it was still bad, very bad, though hilarious if you were a dad. And mildly witty if you happened to have the biggest crush ever on the person who'd told the joke. Which she did.

Oooooooh.

While she'd been pondering, another email had materialised in her inbox.

To: janeeyre2@gmail.com
From: jackbee@hotmail.com
Subject: PS

Excellent eyelashes, btw.
J

Omigod. It *was* him! This was just too much. Carefully moving the laptop aside, Charlotte bum-shuffled herself to a clutter-free part of the bed where she performed a celebratory swoon onto the duvet. (Not bad. She gave herself seven out of ten for style. It had been a little too Jane Austen for her liking—tight bodice rather than Yorkshire-moor-fuelled raw emotion.) Hurriedly, she sat up again. Jack was online now.

Now!

She grabbed the laptop and clicked on *Reply*. Like a magician on the verge of declaring *abracadabra*, she poised her fingertips above the keyboard. She was going to write the best email ever. If Ms Brontë herself had been blessed with a broadband connection instead of pen and ink, she couldn't have done better.

She was going to do it right now.

Just as soon as inspiration struck, that was.

But annoyingly, the perfect witty response hovered just out of reach. The first version was too gushy and the second too dull. The fifth was too heart-on-her-sleeve. The twelfth invited him to the cinema—too forward. The twenty-third too mystic—a detailed analysis of their star-sign compatibility. By the thirtieth version, she was beginning to despair. But by the thirty-seventh, she had it—a masterpiece of brevity and politeness.

To: jackbee@hotmail.com
From: janeeyre2@gmail.com
Subject: Re: PS

Why, thank you.
C

PS Ha ha!

Before she could change her mind and embark upon the thirty-eighth version, Charlotte hit *Send*. Totally spent, she flopped back onto the bed and reached automatically for *Jane Eyre*. In the light of recent events, she would reread the part where Blanche Ingram flaunts herself mercilessly in front of Mr Rochester. She would not check her email every two minutes. A watched inbox never fills up.

She opened The Book.

Like an unwelcome late addition to the Big Brother house, Blanche Ingram burst into Thornfield—and Charlotte was sucked in. Sounds jostled at the edge of her consciousness, adding a contemporary feel to the nineteenth-century events. Moonlight and candlelight . . . *daaa ding diddle-ing, diddle-ing ding DING ding* . . . the rustle of expensive silk . . . a distant car alarm . . . ebony eyebrows and hooded lids . . . the low whirr of a laptop . . . the rhythmic slapping of cards, expertly dealt . . . an exhaust's throaty roar . . . meaningful glances . . . urgent knocking . . . more knocking . . .

Disorientated, she sat up. The knocking was now, not then. And it was happening to her front door. The digits on her alarm clock glowed red.

8:54

It wasn't like Manda to come round this late, especially when they hadn't arranged to meet. But it wasn't unheard of. She remembered with fondness the time Manda had unearthed furry handcuffs in her mum's bottom drawer and galloped straight round to the privacy of Charlotte's room to make gagging noises and splutter how 'bad and wrong' it all was. It had been a brilliant night. Something of *that* ilk would be worth interrupting The Book for.

Charlotte rushed to find out what was going on, but she'd only reached the landing when Mum opened the door to the eager knocker.

'At last,' she said, with what sounded like a heartfelt sigh. 'You got a lift then, did you?'

'Too much paraphernalia to fit in my rucksack,' said a man's voice from the darkened doorway. Why didn't he step forward where Charlotte could *see* him? 'Julie dropped me off. Any excuse to parade around in that flash new car of hers.' He gave a short, humourless laugh.

Charlotte shrank away from the banister into the shadows, much as she imagined a prime suspect might do when an inspector came calling. It never harmed to practise that sort of thing. The most innocent of people were accused of heinous crimes on telly all the time. She crouched in the darkness and watched as the owner of the voice—encased in a thick overcoat and wearing a woolly hat—stomped into the hall.

'Is that the orange car?' Mum giggled like the schoolgirl she wasn't. 'If that were mine, I'd probably be showing off too.'

'Lotus.' The visitor snorted. 'Loads Of Trouble, Usually Serious.' He yanked off his hat and dark, glossy hair sprang into view. 'And what about your carbon footprint?' he continued sternly. 'No, you're better off with a bike.'

Oh, crikey. Had her mother taken up with an environmentalist? Was it goodbye luxurious, white, cushiony toilet paper? Hello recycled, grey, scratchy stuff that salved your conscience at the expense of your bottom?

A gurgling sound rose from the hall. It was Mum—laughing again.

Charlotte was just about to leap from her hiding place to remind everyone concerned that there were two of them in this household and that she'd like to be informed, thank you very much, should a third person be moving in, and what about her strenuous efforts on her mother's romantic behalf—were they to be wasted?—not to mention the near impossibility of going on exotic minibreaks without increasing one's carbon footprint . . . when the man shrugged off his coat to reveal a well-cut suit.

It was Mr Grant.

Of course it was Mr Grant. Who else rode a bike, but was chauffeured around in an orange Lotus? By Julie.

'Here, I brought red,' he said, proffering a bottle. 'Shall we get on with it?'

'*Wow*,' mouthed Charlotte. Talk about blunt.

'Smashing,' said Mrs Penman.

The kitchen door clunked shut, reducing the conversation to a low, useless mumble interrupted by the odd incriminating clink of wine glasses.

Deep in thought, Charlotte crept back to her room. Her list of primary objectives was safely tucked away in her wastepaper bin—no one would think to look for it there. She smoothed flat the flyer, picking off threads of banana innards that were stuck to it. Instantly, they stuck to her fingers instead. Ew.

Objective One: Find Mum suitable Mr Rochester for marriage purposes.

She scrawled a large, flamboyant tick. Job done. Mr Grant was in the kitchen right now, using his glowering, enigmatic charm to seduce Mum in classic Rochester style. Excellent. Although, on second thoughts—and even though she'd personally engineered the whole thing—that wasn't necessarily something she wanted to contemplate for too long. Old people kissing? Bleurgh.

Objective Two: Discover true identity of Blanche Ingram/

orange-Lotus-driving-scarlet-woman/Mr Grant's 'bit on the side'. . .

Another tick, but a smaller one this time. Blanche Ingram's cover was blown. She was . . . drum roll . . . *Julie*! But Julie who? Was she a scarlet woman in an orange car? Or was that just a terrible colour combination? The more Charlotte thought about it, the weirder it seemed that Mr Grant's fancy woman would deliver him into the arms of his true love. Was he tricking them both? She sighed. Julie appeared to have introduced more questions than she answered. But at least Charlotte was getting somewhere.

Objective Three: Convince Jack Burley that I'm not a total fool.

How in Rochester's name was she going to do that? In desperation, she fired off an email.

To: jackbee@hotmail.com
From: janeeyre2@gmail.com

127

Subject: Balls

Don't suppose you'd like to discuss the French essay in the library tomorrow lunch time, would you?
C

She sent her first attempt before she had a chance to change her mind. *Ping!* Off it went.

Almost instantly, she regretted it.

Discussing an essay in a library?

Hey, why hadn't she gone the whole hog and asked him if he fancied visiting a museum of antique paperweights? Or *Swan Lake?*

She hung her head in dismay.

Why was she even bothering? Jack didn't have any sort of romantic notion about her. It was something she'd dreamed up, all by herself. When he'd taken her email address, he was only being polite. And she'd misread that for . . . Well, whatever her romance-addled brain had imagined, it was too late now. She'd invited Jack on the world's dullest date.

Charlotte idly traced her forefinger

on the mouse pad to rouse the laptop from its automatic snooze and began another email. She'd confess all to her best friend. If anyone could help her to see the funny side, Manda would.

CHAPTER FIFTEEN

Mrs Penman seemed to be entirely oblivious to the fact that she owed her daughter a concise description—minus the disgustingly sloppy bits—of the evening's events. At breakfast, she was annoyingly vague, preferring to study her teaching notes instead of elaborating. Every single one of Charlotte's deceptively casual yet so carefully rehearsed questions was met with a monosyllable.

'How did last night go?'
'Good.'
'So what did you do?'
'Work.'
'*Just* work?'
'Yes.'
Casual was getting her nowhere. It

was time to go for the jugular.

'So who was the bloke at the front door with the bottle of red wine who you smuggled into the kitchen before I could check him out?'

This got Mum's attention. Bleary-eyed, she looked up from her overloaded lever-arch file. 'Huh?'

'That bloke,' persisted Charlotte. 'It was Mr Grant, wasn't it?' She didn't wait for confirmation. 'Why did he bring wine?'

Mrs Penman smiled. 'Is that a trick question?' she asked. 'He brought the wine—a lovely *Montalcino*, incidentally—so we could drink it.'

'Aha! I knew it!' exclaimed Charlotte.

'You knew what?' said Mrs Penman pleasantly. For a mum who'd quite likely been swinging from the light shades with Mr Grant all night, she didn't look anywhere near guilty enough. Not guilty in the slightest, actually. Did the woman have *no* morals?

Charlotte went for it. 'And now you're madly in love with him?' She nodded encouragingly, to prompt her suspect. 'Aren't you?'

'Er . . .' For a moment, Mrs Penman looked bewildered. She flushed guiltily. Then she recovered her composure. 'No,' she said firmly. 'No, I'm not. Whatever would give you that idea?'

Charlotte had expected this. Her mother was in denial. (Here, a daft joke about paddling in the world's longest river popped unbidden into her thoughts. She pushed it firmly away. Now was not a time for Dad Jokes.) It was possible that Mrs Penman hadn't realised Mr Grant was in love with her. If that was the case, she must be gentle. 'So what were you doing in the kitchen last night then?' she asked.

'Discussing Ofsted over a civilised glass of wine,' said Mrs Penman. She seemed quite intent on persisting with her feeble explanation, '. . . with Roger and Muriel and Colin.'

What? Who in heaven's name were Roger and Muriel and Colin? Members of the Institute of Dull Names? What had they done to poor, loveable, environmentally friendly Mr

131

Grant? Questions tumbled through Charlotte's mind like flik-flaking gymnasts, until one paused long enough for her to hang on to it. 'What happened to Mr Grant?' she asked quietly.

'Roger?' said Mum. 'Why . . . nothing. Muriel and Colin—you know, Mrs Hook and Colin Jeffries, the music teacher—arrived just after him. We formulated a strategy for Ofsted. And then everyone went home.'

'Roger?' repeated Charlotte. Her thought process had snagged on the very first word. 'Mr Grant's name is Roger?'

'Ye-es,' Mum said, lifting her shoulders and the palms of her hands in a what's-the-problem gesture.

'Not . . . Edward?' asked Charlotte. Mr Grant reminded her so strongly of Edward Rochester that she'd naturally assumed they'd share the same name. To her, the name Edward conjured up dark-eyed passion, intense power . . . It spoke of a strong, stubborn, romantic man who thundered across dark moors on horseback, a man who would stop at

132

nothing to achieve his heart's desire.

Roger was the name of a pet-shop owner.

Mrs Penman shook her head. 'Not Edward,' she said.

'Ranulph? Ralph? Hugh?' pleaded Charlotte. Then, as a last resort, 'Maximilian?'

'Sorry,' said Mum. 'His name's Roger. And he was ever so helpful, you know. We've quite got over our little disagreement.' She laughed lightly. 'Now, as enjoyable as it is to be given the third degree over breakfast, I suggest we leave this until later and get to school.'

*   *   *

'And that's all you got out of her?' asked Manda. 'Mr Grant's first name is *Roger*?' She frowned and shook her head. 'Dreadful.'

'It is, isn't it?' said Charlotte, happy that Manda agreed with her, but surprised that she seemed so crotchety about it. '*Really* dreadful. Who would foist a name like that upon a child

133

when they could have called them Edward instead?'

'No,' muttered Manda. 'I mean that your powers of investigation are dreadful. Forget the haystack—you couldn't find a needle in a sewing box.' She flipped open her French course book and stared angrily at a cartoon drawing of a deliriously happy customs officer and instructions on how to ask him what he liked to do in his spare time.

Charlotte might not be destined for Scotland Yard, but even she could tell that all was not right here. Two things bothered her. One, Manda hadn't replied to last night's momentous email about Jack . . . drum roll . . . Burley. And two, she was totally overreacting about Roger. Even Charlotte didn't think it was *that* bad a name.

So what was up?

Because usually, whenever Charlotte worried and whinged, ranted and stropped, Manda listened calmly, before zapping the problem with a droll comment. And if she couldn't zap it, she joined in with the worrying, whingeing, ranting and stropping, so Charlotte didn't feel isolated. Usually. But not today. Was Manda mixing Charlotte up with some other best friend who thrived on insults? One thing was for certain—she wasn't reading.

'Your book's upside down,' said Charlotte quietly.

There was furious *pfuff* of disgust. Manda spun the book 180 degrees and continued frazzling the page with her death stare.

Convinced now that she'd committed a truly heinous crime, Charlotte ran through a mental checklist of Things Most Likely To Upset Manda.

1. Dropping her in it with parents. (Totally out of the question. No one *ever* did this.)
2. Stealing her boyfriend. (Easy. No boyfriend to steal.)
3. Sharing top-secret cup-size information with boys. (Why would she? Charlotte had some highly sensitive cup-size

information of her own to keep
quiet.)
  4. Revealing that she still ate
     alphabet-shaped spaghetti—and
     liked it. (Charlotte liked it too.)

Which brought her to the last one. The
big one. The Thing That Was More
Likely Than Anything Else In The
World To Upset Manda.

  5. Putting a boyfriend before a
     friend. (Oh, no. She hadn't done
     this. No way. For starters, she
     didn't even *have* a boyfriend.)

'Chas!'
  Her mouth hung open unattractively.
Quite the last person in the world she
expected to be hollering at her was
doing just that.
  'Oy!' shouted Jack.
  'Huh?' Inwardly, she reprimanded
herself for being so DULL. Again.
Jane Eyre, pint-sized queen of
feistiness, would have been zapping
Jack with her prim and passionate
lexicon, cutting and thrusting with witty

phrases, jabbing with punctuation.

She would have done better than 'huh'.

Charlotte stretched her lips across her teeth in a taut smile, watching as Jack threaded his way between the tables towards her. She knew instinctively that Manda's eyes had lifted from the smoking page and— WHAM!—it hit her. She'd already arranged to see Manda at lunch time.

She had double-booked her Best Friend and Some Boy.

With sudden toe-curling, gut-clenching realisation, she knew that Manda *had* got the email about Jack and lunch. And *that* was why she was upset. And Charlotte knew that she should apologise *now*. Before Manda's famous temper went nuclear.

But Jack looked so lovely that even though she *knew* that she should kick-start the grovelling process, Charlotte couldn't drag her eyes away. His artfully tousled hair bobbing slightly as he walked. (Did he use conditioner?) Today, his eyes were the colour of watermelons—cool, luscious, tasty, not to mention a distinct improvement on sludge. Mmm.

'Here,' he said, reaching her at last. (That was the trouble with walking in romantic slow-motion. It took so long to get anywhere.) Proudly, he handed over a messy pile of photocopied pages. 'This is only part of it. You can see the rest in the library, if you like?'

Whoa. Charlotte grasped the sheaf of papers with one hand and curled the fingers of her other hand into her palm. She dug her nails in—hard. Yep, that hurt all right. She was definitely awake.

'Ha,' muttered Manda under her breath. 'And you'll show her your stamp collection too, I suppose.'

Charlotte aimed a deft kick at Manda's shin. Whether she'd double-booked or not, Manda was forgetting the next Thing Most Likely to Upset a Friend.

6. Never get between a friend and a boy.

'Hmm?' Luckily, Jack was too busy demonstrating his Googling prowess to

138

notice the deadly atmosphere. He pointed to the page on the top of her pile. 'Here, I searched for *boules* and then *bowls* and then *balls*—I got eighty and a half million results for that one!'

'What do you want—a medal?' grumbled Manda.

'*Cool!*' said Charlotte loudly, in an attempt to drown out her friend's less than subtle comments. Had he heard the jibe? From his still-happy expression, she didn't think so. 'That's brilliant. Thanks so much. Anyway . . .' As much as she was enjoying the novelty of standing so close to Jack and his so-cute freckles, she had to end this before Manda exploded in a fit of pique. Her eyes flicked around the classroom, gratefully landing on the green plastic clock on the wall. She flinched with feigned surprise. 'Wow! Is that the time?'

Flicking guacamole eyes towards the clock, Jack pushed up his sleeve and then consulted the colossal watch that hugged his wrist. '8:55 am,' he said. 'Spot on.'

'Well, thanks again,' said Charlotte.

'I'll maybe catch up with you la—'

'. . . which means that it's 3:55 in New York, 9:55 in Berlin and,' he pressed a button, '13:25 in Delhi.'

'Excellent—'

'It's 25 degrees Celsius and we're 50 metres above sea level. Oh, and atmospheric pressure is 998 millibars, which probably means rain.'

Charlotte waited a couple of seconds, in case any more data was forthcoming, but Jack was done. He grinned proudly, with the air of a cat that's brought its owner an extremely dead mouse.

'Ahem. Sorry to interrupt,' said Manda, not looking remotely sorry, 'but you're blocking my light. Any chance you could shove off?'

Jack looked uncomfortable. The menace behind Manda's words was impossible to ignore. 'Er . . . right,' he said, scratching his head. 'See you around.' Without even a glance in Charlotte's direction, he turned and strode back to his desk, where he immediately began a loud discussion about the Champions League.

'Thanks,' hissed Charlotte. However cross Manda might be, there was no excuse for this. 'The first chance I get to talk to the *only* boy on my radar and you muck it up. What's your problem, eh?' She dragged the next chair from under the table—its metal feet stuttering noisily across the rubber tiles—and sat down.

'Rule number five.' Each word was spoken with the venom of a James Bond villain.

'But I haven't broken rule number five,' whispered Charlotte. 'I haven't put a boyfriend before a friend because *he's not my boyfriend.*'

'Don't think you're getting out of this on a technicality,' growled Manda. 'We were meant to be having lunch. And you dumped me. *For a boy.* It's obvious there's something going on between you.'

Instantly, Charlotte's insides began to churn like her mum's ice-cream maker. This was it. Jack had declared undying love. He'd just been too shy to tell her himself. 'Is there?' she whispered. 'Does he . . . f-f-fancy me?'

Charlotte had only seen Manda totally freak out on one previous occasion. It had been impressive then and it was spectacular now. 'Me-me-me-me-me-*meeeeeeee*!' she cried. 'That's all you ever want to talk about! You and your piddling, poxy, *insane* obsession with an antique celebrity with bird's-nest hair. It's all about *you*, isn't it? You and Jane Eyre. You're Jane . . . Jane . . . Jane *Airhead*, that's what *you* are. Well, what about *meeeeeeee*?'

The room was silent.

'Ladies.' Mrs Hook had materialised in the classroom doorway. She carefully inserted a cherry-red-tipped finger into her ear and wiggled it gently. 'I'm not sure Miss Stone caught all of that. I suggest you both adjourn to her office and explain just why it's necessary to screech like a harpy when there isn't a drama teacher in sight. Now, before you perforate any more eardrums . . . go!'

They went.

CHAPTER SIXTEEN

'Sorry,' muttered Charlotte, as they shuffled reluctantly along the corridor. 'I mean, I'm *really* sorry. I truly didn't realise I was being so selfish.'

'And self-obsessed,' prompted Manda.

'And self-obsessed.'

'And ginger.'

'And ging— Eh?' Charlotte came to a halt. 'I'm not ginger! Urgh.' Guilt flooded in as a soft-focus image of her auburn sweetheart appeared in her mind.

'Gotcha!' said Manda quietly. She glanced sideways at Charlotte. 'I'm sorry too,' she murmured. 'It's not that I don't like hearing about your bloke and your mum's bloke, but I do wish that every once in a while, perhaps every other blue moon, we talked about mine.'

'*Your* bloke?' said Charlotte. Had her friend been harbouring a secret crush all this time? 'Why didn't you *say*? Of course we can talk about your bloke—we can do it now! Who *is* he?'

Manda mumbled a reply.

'Daniel?' said Charlotte. That's what it had sounded like.

'No . . . *dunno*,' said Manda. 'I mean, he might be called Daniel, but I haven't found him yet so it's probably best if I don't make the search even more difficult by insisting that's his name. I'd be more than happy with an Andrew. Or a Paul. And a Rob would do . . . Just so long as he isn't called Edward Rochester. I've had enough of that name to last me several lifetimes.'

'Sorry . . .' said Charlotte.

'Oh, stop apologising and tell me what's going on,' said Manda briskly. 'I'm sorry I flipped. But all I got from last night's email was that you were dumping me for some ginger boy.'

'He's not ginger!' cried Charlotte.

'Yeah, right.' Manda arched an eyebrow. 'Come on, then. Tell me everything.'

Charlotte told her. Everything. Not that there was much to tell. A dreadful joke about balls. A few silly emails. A dull date in the library that was *so* not happening now that she and Manda had performed their banshee double act.

'So there was no secret plot to dump me in favour of Jack?'

'Never.'

'Good.'

They stopped and faced Miss Stone's office door. Yet more lightly seared salmon-pink paint. Her mind drifting off to more pleasant places at the imminent prospect of being lightly seared herself, Charlotte wondered if the school's painters had gone off fish after decorating the school.

Charlotte rapped quietly on the door. Immediately, it was wrenched open and they faced the spectre of Mrs Pearson. The terrifying school secretary appeared to have been lying in wait, salivating in anticipation of their arrival. 'Yesssss?' she hissed.

'W-we wanted to see Miss Stone,' squeaked Manda.

'Oh, you *did*, did you?' Mrs Pearson bared her teeth. In some circles— probably those frequented by blood-

145

sucking vampires—this may have been called a smile. 'Come on in.' The secretary pointed to a row of wooden chairs that stood to attention against the wall. 'Sssssit.'

They crept into the outer office that Mrs Pearson occupied. And sat.

'I'll tell her you're here.' The secretary showed her fangs again before knocking reverently on the door to the inner sanctum.

'Come!'

Mrs Pearson slipped inside, leaving the door ajar. A low murmuring came from within.

'I hate that,' said Manda.

'What?' replied Charlotte in an undertone. 'The horribly sick feeling you get when you know you're going to be lambasted by someone in a position of authority?'

'It should quite obviously be "come in",' growled Manda. 'It's as bad as saying "Thank" or "Excuse". It's pure laziness—'

'Shhhhhh!' Charlotte put a finger to her lips and glared. Inside the lion's den, the hushed voices had grown louder and satisfyingly indiscreet.

'It must be terribly unsettling . . . moving to a new area, I mean,' said Miss Stone. 'Especially if she doesn't know a soul.'

Who were they talking about? The imminent tongue-lashing instantly forgotten, Charlotte edged forward, hungry for more clues.

'And she doesn't have a job yet, so she's bound to be lonely.'

'But let's face it, who wouldn't follow such a . . . a . . . handsome man to the ends of the earth? I know I would.'

The head teacher's voice was uncharacteristically whimsical. Who *were* they talking about? Someone from *Heat* magazine?

'And teachers work such long hours. It's not like they can switch off when school finishes. There's all that planning and marking and Ofsted only adds to the workload. . . Still, I hear she's going to get herself a car. She wanted a Land Rover Sport but he's told her it has to be a hybrid. You know what he's like about the environment.'

Someone who was lucky enough to

have ensnared a good-looking teacher? (And Lord knows there weren't many of *them*.) Who could it *be*?

'Still, half term's coming up. Roger said that he might take the good lady on a minibreak to Cannes. Get a bit of autumn sun.'

'Marvellous . . .' Mrs Pearson exhaled noisily, before returning to the business in hand. 'Now, shall I bring in the next offenders?'

Charlotte's throat was so dry that she felt as if she were swallowing an entire Victoria sponge. A handsome teacher who just happened to be called Roger? It could only mean one thing.

Mr Grant was *married* !

CHAPTER SEVENTEEN

Never had Charlotte been so angry. Not even when *Jane Eyre* had come tenth—*TENTH!*—in a survey of the nation's favourite books, after *Lord of the Rings*, after *Winnie the Pooh* and after (this one really hurt) *Pride and*

Prejudice. The nation was quite obviously stupid.

How dare Mr Grant? How *dare* he wine and dine her mother—well, wine and whine her, anyway—when all the time he was married to a lovely, unsuspecting woman, who had no idea that her rat of a husband was seeing not one but *two* other women! Because Charlotte wasn't daft. It didn't take a degree in Jumping to Conclusions to work out that the infamous Julie wasn't the French teacher's wife. Poor, deluded Mrs Grant was *thinking* of getting a car—she wasn't swanning around in an orange Lotus. Like *Julie*.

Whatever wrongs Mr Rochester may have committed, he was a total novice compared with Mr Grant. Charlotte had made a terrible mistake when she'd put them both in the apparently-cruel-but-nice-really segment of the Venn diagram.

It was all a horrible mess.

Charlotte hurled the ivory and cappuccino bridesmaid's dress—with a chiffon overskirt and tiny pearls dotting the hem—to the back of her mental wardrobe. There would be no wedding now. She couldn't allow her mother to marry such a despicable man. No, she would put her plans into reverse. If she could bring two people together, it would surely be no problem to push them apart again. She would use the power of suggestion. That would do it. But first, she needed to explain why she and Manda had been sent to the head teacher's office.

*   *   *

Mrs Penman was livid. 'Miss Stone tells me that you were brawling in class. Like *thugs*. What were you *thinking*?'

'Not brawling exactly,' said Charlotte, hoping that a super-soothing voice would bring her mum's volume down. She'd been collared in the main thoroughfare between the Upper and Lower Schools—the perfect spot to be observed by a constantly changing audience. (Nice one, Mum. By home time *everyone* would know that she'd been Stoned.) 'Just one of those everyday discussions that got ever so

150

slightly out of hand,' she said, with a light-hearted laugh, not unlike the sound of a garden water feature. 'We're best of friends again now. Can I go?'

'No,' replied her mum. 'Mrs Hook said you were screeching like banshees. I want to know why.'

'Harpies,' Charlotte corrected her. 'Banshees wail. And it was honestly just a discussion. We fell out. We've made up. End of story.'

'I'm not convinced,' said Mum dubiously. 'What's the punishment?'

'The usual,' she said. 'Lines and litter-picking. Oh, and we have to man, I mean woman . . .' She scratched her head in an attempt to trigger the politically correct verb. 'No, I mean *person* the drinks stall at the next bring-and-buy sale.'

'*Run* the drinks stall?' suggested Mum.

'Yep. Spot on.' Charlotte nodded, praying that the lexical dilemma had sidetracked her mother. 'What are you doing after school?'

'Thinking of a suitable punishment

to add to the list,' Mrs Penman growled. 'But seeing as you ask, I'll also be staying late for an Ofsted meeting. Before I heard about your terrible behaviour, I was going to ask if Manda's mum might have you over for tea. But I'm not sure now. Goodness knows what you might do to each other with knives and forks.'

'Oh, we're fine!' said Charlotte brightly. It was true—they really were. Manda was as intrigued as she was by Mrs Grant's appearance. And now they'd decided to widen the manhunt to include not only a bloke for Mrs Penman and one for Charlotte—there was no news on Jack's current opinion of her, post-fight, so she had to assume the worst—but one for Manda too. Her best mate was so totally on board that she could have been mistaken for a sailor in the Royal Navy.

'Who'll be at the meeting?' she asked casually.

'The usual suspects,' said Mum, thankfully calmer now. 'Why do you ask?'

'Oh, no reason,' replied Charlotte

airily. 'It's just that . . . oh, never mind.'

'What?' Instantly, Mum's suspicions were alerted, just as her daughter had known they would be.

'You probably wouldn't be interested.'

'What?' Louder this time.

Oh, yes. She'd reeled her in like a prize marlin. It was time to bag the catch. 'Well, you won't be mixing with Mr Grant, will you?'

'Of course I will,' said her mum, frowning. 'Why?'

'Oh, nothing.'

'*Why?*'

'I'm not sure he's the sort of person you should be getting involved with, that's all,' said Charlotte. The crowds were thinning now, so they weren't likely to be overheard.

'Why?' Mrs Penman's voice was edged with irritation.

'Mum,' said Charlotte. 'It kills me to tell you this, but . . .'

Her mother leaned forward.

'. . . he's married. To his wife.'

'Really?' Her mother leaned back and laughed. 'Well, I didn't expect he'd be married to his great-aunt Frieda,' she said. 'It's not like he's a member of the royal family or something.'

'You knew?'

Mrs Penman looked puzzled. 'Knew he was married? Of course I knew.'

What?

This was a possibility Charlotte hadn't even considered. If someone had accused Mum of cavorting around with married men as if she didn't have a moral in the world, Charlotte would have scoffed at the very idea. Never. She'd be more likely to eat a Happy Meal. 'But you let him come round our house,' she said.

'Ye-e-s.' Mum smiled in the manner of one about to deliver a supremely patronising lecture. She put her arm around Charlotte's shoulder. 'Darling, just because someone's married, doesn't mean that they have to stop seeing other people,' she said. She flushed prettily. 'In fact, darling, there's something we need to talk about. I've been putting it off, waiting for just the right moment, but—'

'No!' cried Charlotte. It was bad

154

enough finding out that her mother thought it acceptable to be a Bit On The Side. The last thing Charlotte wanted was to hear the sordid details too. If she could have flung her arm across her tortured brow and swooned onto a well-sprung object, she would have. It was OK to see two men at the same time? Since when had this ever been the accepted wisdom in their house? Charlotte stared horror-struck at her mother, searching for signs of the woman who'd taught her, amongst many other things:

1. Never to beg, borrow or steal.
2. Never to ask people how old they were, unless they were quite obviously under ten or over seventy.
3. Never to eat the last chocolate at someone else's house (at home, go for it—hence *The Case of the Vanishing Green & Blacks*).
4. Always to give up her seat on the bus if there was a pensioner within spitting distance.

5. Always to include the unpopular child in party games, even if they were smelly.

And she was sure she'd heard something about coveting your neighbour's wife. Or husband. Or Land Rover Sport.

Where was this paragon of virtue now? Gone. In her place was a woman with the scruples of an assassin—a wanton hussy who saw nothing wrong in stealing another woman's man. Vague memories of the fire-and-brimstone vicar who had conducted Auntie Bernice (not a real auntie—but a rather stylish pretend one who Mum knew from way back) and Uncle Fred's wedding floated back to her. Mum had torn Mr and Mrs Grant asunder, that's what she'd done. And from her twinkling eyes, it looked as if she'd enjoyed it.

'Er, well . . . we must talk about it soon, then,' said Mum, looking less sure of herself now. 'But in answer to your question, yes, I'll be seeing Roger tonight. And Muriel and Colin and half the school staff. But I'll make sure that Mr Grant doesn't corrupt me and I won't be late, I promise. I'll come and pick you up from Manda's house at 9pm sharp. By then, I should have had time to devise a firm-but-fair punishment.'

And that was that.

CHAPTER EIGHTEEN

Mum's punishment was inspired and utterly heartless. Charlotte was to read *Pride and Prejudice*. And, as if that wasn't bad enough, she was then to write a short essay entitled *Ten Things I Really Admire About Jane Austen's Work*. Crikey. It was going to be hard enough to find one. (It wasn't that Charlotte didn't *like* Jane Austen. It was more that, with both feet firmly planted in the Charlotte Brontë camp, it felt like the worst type of betrayal to compliment Austen, no matter how brilliantly ironic and witty she might be.)

And meanwhile, the runaway Ofsted train kept steaming down the track, hurtling ever closer to the school. It was getting closer. And closer. Then . . . *toot*! It was here.

*   *   *

Mum looked sick.

Briefly putting her moral judgements to one side—even adulterers needed a word of comfort every now and again—Charlotte patted her mother's shoulder. 'Are you OK?' she asked.

'I can't even remember who wrote *Nineteen Eighty-four*, never mind how to teach it,' replied Mrs Penman. 'I didn't sleep; I can't eat; I've put three layers of deodorant on and I'm still sweating. Do I seem OK to you?' Her crazed eyes stared nervously out of a sheet-white face.

'But your hair looks lovely,' said Charlotte, deciding to concentrate on the positive. It was probably best not to mention that her under-eye circles were so bad she looked as if she'd gone three rounds with the World

Heavyweight Champion. 'You're bound to get extra points for style.' She smiled encouragingly.

Mum groaned. 'I hope you're right,' she said.

The Ofsted inspectors were going to spend three days at the school. During that time, they would watch *everything*—and say nothing. The verdict came later. A week or so after their departure, a report would arrive at the school either congratulating the school on a job well done or providing the head teacher with a list of improvements to be carried out with all due haste—or else. It all sounded very scary. And very dull. But in the event, it all happened very quickly.

By an unspoken agreement, pupils decided to cooperate with the teachers—after all, they were likely to get it in the neck afterwards if they didn't. Every question was met with a sea of waving hands, not necessarily followed by the correct answer, but hey, the teachers couldn't have everything.

As for the Ofstedders themselves,

Charlotte was amazed to discover that they looked, well, *normal*. She'd half imagined they'd arrive sporting pointy hats and black-and-white-striped tights in the style of the Wicked Witch of the West. But they wore tweed, brogues and—in one case—a pink shirt. What they didn't do was smile—not in public anyway. Although Manda claimed to have seen one of them sniggering behind the bike sheds when he read his po-faced colleague's notes.

Charlotte's greatest feat was correctly answering a question on simultaneous equations—in truth, a matter of luck rather than mathematical ability, but how were the inspectors to know? Yet even while she sat bolt-upright in class, trying to summon up enthusiasm for the whole tedious affair, her thoughts were elsewhere. About 3.5 metres to the right, to be precise. Because, after The Brawl—as she and Manda now referred to it—there had been no more deliciously exciting moments with Ol' Green Eyes. He'd nodded to her a couple of times, but that was it. No lunch. No emails. No 'Chas'. No hands entwined in the popcorn bucket on the back row of the cinema . . . Especially not that.

'So what are you going to do?' asked Manda on the last afternoon of 'Orrible Ofsted, as it had quickly become known. They were leaning against the wall at the edge of the school yard, pretending to be absorbed in a copy of *Physics Is Fun!* (The author of the book certainly thought so, anyway.) There was a sense of demob hysteria in the air. Everyone knew that the Ofsted inspectors were about to leave and there were high hopes that the last two days of school before the half-term holiday would combine the comforting *ching* of Connect 4 and the relaxation of Rummy—the only card game currently allowed after the bleeding knuckles of the end-of-summer-term's Chase-the-Ace whack-athon. As Miss Stone said, if the law forbade teachers to rap pupils' knuckles, then she wasn't going to allow them to have all the fun by doing it to each other with lethal stacks of

161

razor-edged playing cards.

'What am I going to do?' repeated Charlotte. 'Dunno. I'm not quite sure how it happened the first time, so how could I do it again?'

'You could try "aloof",' suggested Manda.

'And make him think that I hate him? Yeah, that'd work,' said Charlotte.

Manda shook her head. 'Nah. It's the oldest trick in the book. Treat 'em mean—'

'You sound like my grandma,' muttered Charlotte. 'If he was keen in the first place, how can I be sure being rotten won't ruin things totally this time?'

'That's the beauty of it,' said her friend. 'You won't, thus generating instant *frisson*. And that can only help. Trust me.'

Manda seemed so completely convinced by her own unfathomable logic that Charlotte began to believe her. She pictured herself gazing into the middle-distance when Jack asked to borrow a protractor, haughtily refusing his offer to share the Twix from his lunch box . . . 'Come on,' she said, nudging Manda with her shoulder. 'You can tell me. You must have stamped on some bloke's ego to be so sure it works.'

'Nope. Absolutely, totally untried and untested!' Manda announced brightly. 'Don't get me wrong,' she added. 'I *am* convinced of its success, but I thought you could give it a test run. I wouldn't want to banjax my own chances, would I?' She raised one of her bendy eyebrows. 'Think about it.'

Charlotte's howl of protest was drowned out by the school bell. But as they trudged back inside, destination History, she found herself mulling over Manda's idea. Perhaps it wouldn't do any harm to lure the delectable Jack by making herself less of a friendly puppy and more of an Ice Queen.

It worked for Greta Garbo.

CHAPTER NINETEEN

And then they were gone.

The Ofstedders scurried away to wreak havoc elsewhere, leaving teachers and pupils to muddle through the few days that remained until half term. Feebly, the teachers tried to summon the energy to instil a few more facts into their charges, but they were easily distracted. Lessons descended into mild chaos, while the staff stared blithely on in a blissful state of couldn't-care-less-ness, having given their brains an early holiday. Only the maths teacher retained a modicum of order with her photocopied Sudoku grids and frenzied games of Fizz Buzz. The maths spods had never had it so good.

Charlotte treated Jack to her iciest glares and her coldest shoulder. As October drew to a close, the weather obliged by smothering all outdoor surfaces with glistening frost. Was Jack bothered? Not a bit of it. He didn't look even remotely chilly, being far too busy talking about his half-term escape to sunnier climes.

That was it, then.

Over, before it had really begun.

Not that Charlotte had ever believed that it had started in the first place. She had to face facts. She wasn't the sort of girl who ensnared boys with a wink and a dropped handkerchief. And she certainly wasn't the sort of girl who ever got the coolest boy in class. She was the sensible one. The bookworm with the big nose.

She should get back to worrying about her mum's loose morals.

*　　　*　　　*

'And you won't give Manda's parents a hard time?' said Mum, nearing the end of her pre-sleepover grilling.

'No, of course not.' Charlotte had switched to auto-response mode twenty minutes earlier and no longer knew what she was promising not to do. But as long as the rules didn't mention stupid make-up, chocolate and minimal sleep, she'd be in the clear. 'And where are you going?' she asked.

Mrs Penman suddenly developed an unconvincing interest in the contents of her handbag. 'I told you,' she said, rifling through old bus tickets and empty chewing gum packets. 'I wouldn't normally do it, not with Mum and Dad coming tomorrow. I should be dousing the place with bleach and stuffing all our tat into the loft . . .' Her eyes darted to and fro at the mess that had built up over the last week. And then she lifted her chin defiantly. 'But I've been invited out for a drink . . . to, er, celebrate the end of the inspection.' She gave a quick smile. 'That hair slide suits you.'

Charlotte was a past master at changing the subject. She was hardly about to allow her own mother to get away with it. 'Didn't you do that on Wednesday?' she asked. 'How many times do you need to celebrate?'

Her mother plucked a tiny mirror from the handbag and began applying vampish lipstick. 'Hmm?' she said distractedly.

It was embarrassing, really. Mrs Penman was so transparent that her skin might as well be made of cling film. 'Will Mr Grant be there?' Charlotte demanded sternly.

The lipstick shot off course, smearing across her mum's cheek. Mum scrubbed at it with a fluffy tissue. 'Er, no—yes, I mean,' she said. 'The thing is . . .' She took a deep breath. 'Do you remember that I said there was something we needed to talk about? Well, it's *someone*, really.'

Charlotte froze. Not this, *again*? She didn't want to hear about Mr Grant, the two-timing rat. And she wouldn't. 'It'll have to wait, Mum,' she said, her voice stonier than Brighton beach.

Mum nodded sadly. 'Whenever you're ready, pet,' she said and popped the top back on her lipstick, wincing as she heard it squish beneath. 'Must remember to wind it down next time . . .' she mumbled to herself. 'Are you ready to go?'

Charlotte nodded. Phew. That was close.

But the strange thing was, she

couldn't quite bring herself to discuss her mum's infidelities with Manda. She didn't think she could have borne the unspoken disapproval in her friend's eyes when she denounced her own mother as a floozy. Besides, it felt horribly disloyal.

But she needn't have worried. Manda didn't give a stuff about Mrs Penman's whereabouts anyway. She shrugged at Charlotte's elaborate lies detailing the night—warm wine, Mecca bingo, chicken in a basket—that her mum had in store. 'Great. Now, what are we doing first? Watching *Dirty Dancing* or testing my new spot plasters?'

*   *   *

On Saturday morning, Charlotte's head was fuzzy and her mouth tasted unpleasantly of an unidentifiable stale sweetness. For a moment, she couldn't remember why. Was this what a hangover felt like? If so, she would sign up for Teetotallers Anonymous at the very first opportunity. Her brain cleared. No . . . this was the aftermath of the contraband popcorn at 1am, followed by a cursory swipe of the toothbrush. Bleurgh.

She reached out and prodded Manda's sleeping form with her forefinger.

'Noooo!' cried her friend. 'Not the Brussels sprouts!'

'It's me,' said Charlotte, obscurely reminded of Jack's green eyes. The memory made her feel sad.

Manda's eyelids flipped open. 'Oh . . . er, cheers.' She licked her lips and grimaced. 'Did we raid the drinks' cabinet?'

Charlotte shook her head without bothering to lift it from the pillow.

'Then why does my mouth taste like Bailey's and Crème de Menthe?'

'Popcorn and toothpaste.'

'Oh.' Manda screwed up her face.

Pushing herself up on one elbow, Charlotte slowly became aware that every millimetre of her tired body felt sluggish. Her jaws ached from chewing unsuitable foodstuffs. Her inner thighs ached from the scissor legs they'd done in time to Mr McNab's ancient Cindy Crawford exercise video. (Why he owned such a thing was beyond them. His muscles wobbled rather than rippled, so he obviously never pranced along with Cindy himself.) As for her poor eyelashes, they were so heavy that she could hardly pull them apart. She rubbed one eye, realising blearily that her lids were actually glued together with super-thick mascara.

From behind the miniature prison bars of her rock-hard lashes, she surveyed the room. Totally trashed. The alarm clock's digits glowed luminous green against the autumnal gloom of morning. She squinted. It was 9:17. 'Just in time for rubbish telly,' she observed. A supremely lazy morning stretched enticingly ahead of them.

'Excellent,' said Manda. She turned over and buried her head under the duvet, remarking bizarrely, 'Wake me up when the cookery starts.'

As the clock flicked to 9:18, the movement dislodged a thought from the recesses of Charlotte's mind. She had the uncomfortable feeling that there was something she was meant to be doing. Right now. She considered random possibilities as she scrabbled among last night's carnage for the remote.

Walk the dog?

She didn't have one.

Do homework?

Not on the *first* day of the holidays.

Hmmm. No sign of the remote. Instead, she grabbed a handful of make-up remover tissues and set to work on her face, marvelling at her lighter-than-air lashes. Regrettably, her new and improved vision made the room look messier than ever. Thank heavens it wasn't hers. Her grandmother was a stickler for—amongst many other things—abnormally high levels of tidiness. Just one glance at this chaos and a defibrillator would have to be applied to her magnificent bosom.

Her grandparents.

They were arriving today.

No, worse than that. They were arriving this morning.

Emitting a strangled wail, Charlotte

wriggled out of her sleeping bag, struggled into her jeans and began flinging belongings into her suitcase. She had to get home before the grandparents arrived and before Grandma gathered enough ammunition with which to bombard her for their entire painful stay.

There was a muffled groan from beneath the duvet. 'Can you keep the noise down? *Some* of us had a late night.'

Charlotte snapped the clasp closed on her suitcase and then realised that she was still dressed in her pyjama top. No time to change now. She looked enviously at her cocooned friend and smiled wickedly. 'Does nail varnish come out of carpets easily or do you need to cut the tufts out to get rid of it completely?' she asked.

'*What?*' Manda sprang upright. '*Where?* Is it bad?' She blanched. 'It's not Mum's Rouge Noir, is it . . . ?' She stopped, registering the broad smile on Charlotte's face. 'You rotten—'

''Bye!' Charlotte dragged the suitcase through the doorway and bounced it down the stairs, ignoring the wails of protest that emitted from Manda's room.

Mr McNab poked his head round the kitchen door. 'Not staying for breakfast, pet? Can't I tempt you with a lovely bowl of Sugar Puffs? We got them specially,' he added proudly. 'I remembered they were your favourite.'

'Ooh . . . er . . . thanks!' said Charlotte fumbling with the door lock. 'But I can't stay. I have to go home and, er . . . tidy my room.' She cringed inwardly. How feeble did that sound? Her mouth began to water—she hadn't eaten Sugar Puffs since Mum had banned sugary cereals and despite the late-night sugar rush, her stomach was growling for them now.

Manda's dad nodded approvingly. 'Marvellous attitude,' he said. 'Shan't keep you.' He flipped the lock and swung the front door open. 'Off you pop.'

Remembering her manners a millisecond too late, Charlotte thanked the front door for having her. And then she turned and ran, the tiny plastic

173

wheels of the suitcase clickety-clacking over the uneven pavement like a high-speed train. Home was only two streets away. She covered the distance in under three minutes—a personal record, even without the thunderous baggage.

From outside, the house seemed tranquil. Good. The grandparents were not skilled in the art of speaking quietly, so they must be still on their way. Charlotte rumbled up the path and let herself in. She stood the suitcase upright. All was quiet.

'Mu-um?' There was an answering scuffle from upstairs, but it didn't sound like frantic cleaning. Perhaps Mrs Penman had done the honours already. Charlotte shrugged and—pausing to kick off her shoes—padded through to the kitchen.

She stopped dead.

A scene of romantic devastation lay before her, incriminating evidence littering every surface. Two empty wineglasses, stained vixen red. A drunken candle, its hardened waxy dribbles pinpointing the exact moment

174

that the room was vacated. (Charlotte shuddered.) It got worse. Half a bag of pasta, an empty can of tomatoes and—in the kitchen bin—a damp, saggy mozzarella packet. Sprinkles of oregano were everywhere.

These were the ingredients for Mum's favourite meal. She'd been out to impress—but not with her dishwashing skills. Dirty dishes and scummy water filled the sink.

This was the beginning of an evening of seduction. And if this was the beginning, where had it ended?

Ker-thump! Charlotte whirled to see the front door quivering in its frame. Adrenalin pumping, she hurtled through the hall. It was Mr Grant—it had to be. Fresh from her mum's boudoir, lipstick decorating the collar of last night's shirt . . . One night she'd been away. And look what had happened! The French teacher had skulked back here after the staff do and drunk wine and eaten pasta and tomatoes and . . . and . . . and now he was running back to his wife. She had to stop this before it went any further!

175

Her sweaty fingers fumbled and slipped on the awkward handle as she struggled to turn it, reminding her of a supremely scary dream where she'd been escaping from a nasty fate and the door handle had turned to butter. Luckily, this one stayed firm. She wrenched it open.

'Darling!'

Lips painted the colour of raw liver puckered and swooped, planting a triumphant *mwah* on her cheek.

'Argghhh—' Charlotte couldn't help it—the sound slipped out before she had a chance to register the fact that this wasn't Mr Grant or the postman or a phantom snogger. It was someone much scarier than that.

It was her grandmother.

CHAPTER TWENTY

Grandma drew back from Charlotte's wild-eyed expression as if she'd been stung. She glanced quickly at her granddaughter's second-best jeans and smoothed bejewelled hands over her own immaculate turquoise and gold outfit. Her hair was a smooth ice-cream swirl of silver. As usual. It never looked anything less than perfect. Even first thing in the morning, Grandma looked like she'd just stepped from the Glamorous Grandmother Competition catwalk.

'I'm *so* sorry,' said Charlotte earnestly. 'You surprised me, that's all.' She leaned forward and kissed the powdery cheek that smelled overpoweringly of lavender, onions and Chanel No 5. 'It's lovely to see you. How was your journey?'

Grandma sniffed. 'It would have been better if your grandfather hadn't taken the scenic route.' She looked around regally before screeching, '*Alfred!*'

'Here, dear,' said Grandad. He struggled up the path from the ancient Jag with two large suitcases. 'Charlotte!' he said, looking her up and down as if surprised she wasn't still in a pushchair. 'My, haven't you grown—'

'Where's your mother?' Grandma

barked.

'Hmm?' Charlotte raised her eyebrows, playing for time. She still had to change her pyjama top, but she'd caught the unmistakeable sound of the shower gurgling into action, which meant that Mum was nowhere near ready to face the music. So Charlotte couldn't escape just yet. 'Oh, she's just putting the finishing touches to her face,' she said brightly. Yeah, right. Scrubbing away all evidence of last night's debauchery, more like. 'Would you care to come through to the living room and make yourselves at home?' she said politely. 'I'll make you both a lovely cup of tea.'

Warily, Grandma followed her into the house, gesturing for her husband to bring the luggage. He obeyed, sinking into a squishy armchair with a contented *oof*. His wife perched on the sofa and winced. 'Alfred?' she said sharply. 'Did you bring my orthopaedic cushion?'

'It's in the car, Olivia,' said Grandad.

'Now, you know I can't sit on this dreadful sofa without it,' she said. 'Not with my back.'

'I'll go and get it, dear.' He pulled himself out of the armchair and winked at Charlotte, who edged towards the door.

'Remember, I only drink Lapsang Souchong!' Grandma called after her. 'Anything else gives me dreadful indigestion.'

'Ha. Wind, she means,' muttered Grandad. 'But better an empty house than a bad tenant, eh?' He nudged Charlotte, who giggled and scurried towards the kitchen to tackle the mess. She was just closing the dishwasher door when guilty feet padded down the stairs and into the living room.

'Mother, how lovely to see you! I thought you weren't arriving until eleven.'

Even at this distance, Charlotte recognised the forced jollity in Mum's voice. It didn't sound like *she'd* had much sleep either. Charlotte tutted. She really shouldn't be witnessing such behaviour. It was a sad state of affairs when a person needed a PG certificate in their own house, and even sadder when the person responsible for dishing out the parental guidance was quite clearly *incapable* of guiding anyone, given her recent behaviour. Charlotte would quite likely need counselling to deal with this whole sordid affair. She could see the headlines in dentist-waiting-room chat magazines now:

ABANDONED WIFE SEEKS SOLACE IN
ARMS OF GRUMPY OLD
TWO-TIMING CHEAT.
DAUGHTER CLAIMS PARTIAL
RESPONSIBILITY, CITING 19TH
CENTURY SIDEBURNS AS CAUSE.

'Stand up straight, dear!' Grandma's command instantly transformed the two interior walls between the living room and the kitchen to tissue paper. She would have been no good in the Secret Service, but she'd have made an excellent foghorn. 'I see you've moved the shepherdess piece. Didn't you like it?'

'Shepherdess?' said Mum uncertainly. 'Oh, the china doll!'

180

'Shepherdess,' corrected Grandma.

'Er . . . yes, I'm sure it's here somewhere. It's one of my favourites.'

Lies now. Charlotte shook her head at the demise of her mum's good character. She dropped a fishy-smelling teabag into the bone china mug they reserved for Grandma. The china doll was on top of the cistern in the toilet. And Mum knew exactly where it was because she'd balanced the figurine there herself while sounding off loudly about its sheer ugliness.

The front door clunked shut.

'Dad!' cried Mrs Penman, apparently grateful for the distraction. 'Good drive?'

Charlotte picked up the tray of tea things and made her way slowly towards the awkward gathering in the living room, her coat still buttoned up to hide her pyjamas. These uncomfortable visits took place twice a year, while she and Mum returned the favour during the summer holidays and at Christmas. (Grandma refused point-blank to spend the festive season anywhere other than her own home.

The one time Mum had made a stand—she and Charlotte had stayed home and spent the *entire* marvellous day in front of the telly, eating until they felt sick—they'd been ostracised until Easter.) The get-togethers were pretty much identical in pattern: initial politeness morphing into stilted conversation, which rapidly descended into accusation and recrimination. The visitors went home in high dudgeon. Usually a day early. And then they did it all again three months later.

It was like being in a bad play that the critics refused to condemn.

'*Here* you are!' exclaimed Grandma, licking her lips as thirstily as if she'd just spent three days in a desert instead of forty minutes on the dual carriageway.

'Here I am,' agreed Charlotte, her eyes lowered to avoid meeting eyes with Mum. She set down the tea tray on the coffee table and wondered fleetingly why it was never a coffee tray or a tea table. 'Now, I've brought milk, sugar, sweeteners, spoons and a jug of hot water. I think that's everything. Do please help yourselves.' Yep, they were still firmly settled in the initial-politeness phase. She'd enjoy it while it lasted.

Grandma peered imperiously over the rims of her half-moon glasses. 'Oh,' she said, packing infinite disappointment into the solitary syllable. 'You don't have brown sugar. Tut, tut, Linda. I'm on the Atkins' now. Only natural ingredients for me, I'm afraid.'

'But the Atkins' Diet means that you can't *eat* sug—' began Charlotte. A frown from Mum silenced her and she scowled back.

They locked eyes for a second, before Mum broke contact.

'Hmm?' Grandma looked blissfully unaware of the tension in the air—and the meaning of the word *diet*. 'I'll have a spoonful of runny honey instead,' she announced. 'And pop in a sweetener while you're at it.'

'I'll go,' Mum offered quickly. She scooted out of the room.

'How about you, Grandad?' asked Charlotte. 'Would you like a splash of camel's milk?'

Her grandfather rumbled with low laughter. 'Just semi-skilled for me, thanks,' he said, laughing at his own joke. 'No sugar—I'm sweet enough.'

Soon the only sounds were the ticking of the carriage clock and the slurp of hot liquid being sucked through false teeth. A full thirty seconds of bliss.

'Lovely,' said Grandad, setting down his cup. 'Got yourself a chap yet?' he asked.

'Er . . .' said Charlotte.

'Wha—?' began her mum.

The two responses hung in the air like accidental burps at a posh dinner party. But Grandad bumbled on regardless, sensing that there was gossip to be had. 'I hope he treats you well,' he chuckled to no one in particular. 'Tell him that I'll string him up otherwise. Ha ha haaaa!' He raised his fists and punched the air softly.

'Oh, Alfred,' said Grandma. 'You know I don't like violence.'

Charlotte gritted her teeth into a forced smile and stared stubbornly at the floor. Which of them was Grandad talking to? Had he somehow guessed that her mum had someone on the scene for the first time in eight years? Or was it simply the same mortifying question that he fired at Charlotte every time he saw her?

'Dad, stop it,' said Mum quietly, apologetically almost. 'You're embarrassing her. Charlotte is much too interested in her studies at the moment to be thinking about boys. Aren't you, pet? You'd rather be reading *Jane Eyre* than looking for your own Mr Rochester, wouldn't you?'

No! Actually I've been looking for your *Mr Rochester. I wasn't to know that he was a crazy, bigamist environmentalist with a wife locked away at home, was I? And I've been so busy concentrating on your love life that* my *Mr Rochester thinks that I've given him the cold shoulder and will never come near me again. Ever!*

Everyone was staring at her and, for one electrifying moment, Charlotte thought that she'd spoken the words aloud. She tried to remember the

185

question that had provoked her silent outrage. The three adults were clearly waiting for a response. 'Suppose so,' she mumbled, hoping that this would satisfy them.

It did. And Mum appeared to be off the hook too. She flashed an appreciative glance, which Charlotte ignored. She wasn't ready to forgive her wanton behaviour just yet. Or to listen to her guilty secrets.

'Do you have a cleaner?' asked Grandma, abruptly changing the subject.

Mum laughed guiltily. (She'd spoken longingly and at length about the many benefits of a cleaner only the week before and seemed on the verge of submitting. But she couldn't admit that to her mother.) 'Of course not,' she replied haughtily, as if she'd been asked whether she used shop-bought pastry. 'A cleaner . . . Imagine that!'

Grandma ran her finger along the Venetian blind and examined the tip. 'Thought not,' she said.

Her granddaughter relaxed. They were back on safe ground.

CHAPTER TWENTY-ONE

For Charlotte, the next few days stretched ahead endlessly. She and Mum still weren't talking properly, but were communicating via nods and grunts. And then there were Olivia and Alfred . . .

Having her grandparents to stay was rather like harbouring dangerous criminals. Charlotte couldn't let them come into contact with the locals for fear of incident. She had to watch them closely to make sure they didn't uncover hidden ornaments or incriminating evidence of unsavoury activities (her mother's activities, naturally) because Grandma wasn't above blackmail, emotional or otherwise. And she had to treat them with kid gloves—one wrong word and anything might happen.

All she had to do was keep them happy.

Easy.

No, really, it was. Charlotte's

technique was 100 per cent foolproof. If she could have patented it, she would have made a fortune. So, as the first day of the visit drew to a close, she sat at her grandmother's feet while trying not to look too far up her cavernous nostrils and delicately dropped the question guaranteed to charm.

'What was it like in the Olden Days, Grandma?'

It was a beautiful moment. All thoughts of housework and china shepherdesses fled from Olivia Lawson's brain, chased by the rose-tinted memories of her perfect youth.

Grandad was too quick for her. 'There was no *Big Brother*,' he interrupted wistfully. He was a big fan. 'And no *Top Gear* either.'

His wife ignored him. 'Well . . .' she began, wedging the orthopaedic cushion firmly behind her bottom and settling herself deeper into the armchair. She was ready for the long haul. 'It was *so* much better than nowadays.'

'Really?' Her granddaughter had

rather counted on this. Just imagine if her grandmother were a fan of iPhones and broadband like Grandad. Such an anomaly was bound to do something major, like upset the space-time continuum in a galaxy far, far away.

'Oh, yes,' continued Grandma. 'People were so much more polite then, there was no graffiti, we left our front doors wide open all day—'

'Not in winter, we didn't,' mumbled Grandad. 'Too blinking cold.'

'Yes, because we had none of this global warming nonsense,' said Grandma, as if the environment were now supplying free central heating to the ungrateful wretches of the twenty-first century. 'We were properly cold, you know. We had real winters. Really *freezing*.' She wriggled her toes in the heat of the gas fire.

'Brilliant.' Charlotte moved on before her grandmother had the chance to embark on her favourite topic: eiderdowns versus duvets. 'And what about when you met Grandad? Was it just like when people go out with each other now?'

Zoof!

There went the blue touchpaper. Time for the fireworks.

Grandma didn't disappoint. 'No!' she squawked. 'We did things properly. None of this speed dating! We—we—we *courted*, that's what we did. Your grandad called round on a Thursday evening to take me to the pictures or for a walk in the park. Sometimes, we'd go for a fish supper. We knew how to behave back then.'

So much for flower power and the Rolling Stones. Charlotte's grandparents must have opted for *1960s Lite: for non-rebellious teenagers (with bonus manners).*

'Zzzz.' Grandad had fallen asleep.

Lucky thing.

Charlotte looked at the clock and wondered when was the earliest she could plead coursework and escape to her room.

*   *   *

Chas! Chas! Chaaaaaas!

The insistent cry chipped away at the

outer edges of Charlotte's dream until she awoke with a start. She'd fallen asleep on top of her duvet, worn out by too much drama and too little sleep. Now she sat bolt upright. Someone was calling to her across the rooftops, screeching her name as if it was the last sound they would ever utter and she were the last person on Earth who could save them from, say, a burning building or eternal damnation or a cross-eyed knife-thrower.

Chas! Chas!

Blearily, she tried to recognise the voice. It was *so* familiar. As sleep faded, she recalled that only one person ever called her this. Not Charlotte, not Charlie, not Lottie, but Chas. Was it really *him*?

Chaaaa. Caaaa! Caaark!

No, it was a seagull.

Disappointment descended like sea mist. Of course it wasn't Jack. She'd stupidly played hard to get and he'd returned the favour by ignoring her. Although—and this had to be even stupider than the time she'd walked into an airborne swing—she had the oddest feeling that the manic seagull had been trying to get in touch . . . trying to tell her something.

No, that was just too silly even for Charlotte. She'd been reading *Jane Eyre* too much. Again.

Downstairs, it was ominously silent. But Charlotte was in no mood for a reconnaissance mission to assess casualties. She grabbed the gently humming laptop from the desk and checked her email instead. Three new messages: one from Catherine in Canada, one from Dad and one from— What? No . . . Could it be? It was! A new message from *Jack*! And it was dated Thursday when *she* thought they'd been incommunicado. Hadn't they? All at once, her heart was thumping so loudly she could hear it. She tingled from head to foot. Her extremities buzzed. Was this what an electric shock felt like?

With a trembling finger, she clicked the mouse pad.

To: janeeyre2@gmail.com
From: jackbee@hotmail.com

Subject: Rebel

Wow. Visiting Stone's office? Not sure my mum will approve of you now . . .
J

She breathed in sharply. Did this mean . . . ? Did he . . . ? Would he . . . ? It was no good. She couldn't take it in. Or think in longer sentences.

She gazed distractedly at the bass guitarist on the back of her door. Was it her imagination or had he suddenly turned a bit, well . . . ugly? If only his eyes were a different colour. Watermelon green—that would be nice. And his dyed-black hair would benefit from a touch of chestnut.

Chestnut?

Charlotte nodded sagely. It was time to admit the truth. She knew it. Everyone else knew it. Jack certainly knew it.

The boy was ginger, all right? Not chestnut, but ginger.

And she'd decided she rather liked it.

CHAPTER TWENTY-TWO

But despite Charlotte's boundless joy over the renewed email contact, there was still The Mum Situation to be dealt with.

More than anything, Charlotte hated falling out with her mother. Neither of them had spoken about the post-romantic evidence strewn about the house. Or the fact that Mum was having it away with a rude, philandering eco-warrior. But after a solid twenty-four hours of hard stares and little else, masked thankfully by the endless twittering of the grandparents, she was starting to miss their cosy chats. Generously, Charlotte decided to make a concession about the sideburned one by downgrading her requirement of a copy of the decree nisi to proof of a trial separation between Mr and Mrs Grant. She couldn't say fairer than that.

The morning after the email before, she bounced into the kitchen, determined to get it sorted. Mum was there already, pretending to bake homemade muffins, but actually just taking them out of a packet and popping them under the grill.

There was an awkward silence during which Charlotte heard her grandparents bickering in the living room about the best way to make a pot of tea. You had to warm the pot first, said Grandma. And you should aim for a colour somewhere between orange and beige. So *this* was where Mum got her obsession with the correct shade for coffee.

Charlotte began her rehearsed speech. 'Look—'

But Mum pulled rank. 'Grandma and Grandad want to take you to a garden centre this morning,' she interrupted gaily. 'Why don't you go and enjoy yourself? I've got some things to sort out.' She clasped her hands together and leaned forward confidentially. 'I know things have been a bit strange recently. Ofsted hasn't helped. And I've had other . . . *things* on my mind. But I'll sort everything out and we'll talk soon. Right?'

'Right.' Charlotte gave a sensible nod. Calm. She had to stay calm. Whooping with joy would send Mum scuttling to the nearest bookshop instead of unravelling the tangled mess of her adulterous love life. She'd have her head in a dodgy, unreadable classic before you knew it. *Tristram Shandy* probably. Charlotte chose her words carefully. 'A garden centre . . . cool.' She couldn't think of anything worse. But if it meant that her mother was contemplating dumping Mr Grant and becoming a trustworthy member of society once more, then it was worth it.

*   *   *

After ninety minutes of the Gardeners' Emporium, Charlotte was on the verge of committing planticide.

The garden centre was the size of three football pitches and, according to Grandad, stuffed to the gunwales (whatever gunwales were—a type of aubergine?) with the best *Osmanthus delavayi* and *Skimmia japonica* he'd ever seen. Charlotte wasn't convinced. They just looked like shrubs to her.

'Look at that *pieris*!' cried Grandma. 'It's huge! It's the biggest one I've ever seen!'

Charlotte's jaw dropped open unattractively. She'd known it would happen sometime, that her grandparents would start shouting rude words at inappropriate moments, but she hadn't expected it *this* early. They hadn't begun to dress in head-to-foot beige yet. She shushed so hard that she dribbled.

'What?' said her grandmother, wide-eyed with innocence. 'Wipe your chin, dear. It *is* a marvellous pieris, you know.' She pointed to a nondescript bush. 'Look at the beautiful variegated leaves.'

'Oh,' said Charlotte, her cheeks hot. A pieris was a plant. Of course it was. 'Right.' Now, where was the nearest venus flytrap? She needed one to open up and swallow her whole.

Her grandmother tinkled with ladylike laughter. 'Oh, dear . . .' she crowed loudly. 'You didn't think I said . . .? Ha ha! Bert, she thought I said *p*—'

Charlotte stuck her fingers in her ears.

*　　　*　　　*

The stale reek of hydrangeas cloaked everything apart from the vile-smelling cardboard tree swinging from the rear-view mirror. By the time they parked up—Grandad neatly scraping his wheel rims along the kerb—Charlotte didn't know what she longed for more: sensational revelations or fresh air.

'Surprise!' sang Grandma, pointing to the pale, papery lilac flowers. They're to thank you and your mother for having us to stay.' She leaned closer. 'Don't you think hydrangeas are nicer than those wishy-washy lilies your mother buys? So much more colour. We decided to treat you both to a plant rather than cut flowers so they last longer.' She wafted the deathly aroma towards her and breathed deeply. 'Aaaaaah . . .'

'Let's go in,' said Charlotte, before

198

she gagged. 'How about a nice cup of Lapsang Souchong?'

'Oh, not in the afternoon, dear,' replied Grandma. 'I only drink Earl Grey after three o'clock.'

'You go and pop the kettle on, sweetie pie,' said Grandad softly. 'I'll bring in the flowers.'

Charlotte smiled gratefully and made a run for it. Mum was closing the oven door on a bubbling shepherd's pie of epic proportions when she burst into the kitchen. 'Well?' she gasped.

'Hello, pet,' Mrs Penman smiled calmly.

Had she reformed already? Her smile didn't look like it belonged to a wanton adulteress. But appearances could be deceptive.

'Well?' asked Charlotte eagerly. 'What's the big announcement?'

Mum took a breath.

Charlotte craned forward.

Mum breathed out again.

Charlotte had rather hoped that the expulsion of air would happen *after* the revelations. 'Mum?' she prompted gently.

A guilty flush illuminated Mum's cheeks before the words exploded from her. 'I've met someone!' She spoke boldly, as if expecting dissent. 'He . . . he . . . he . . .'

'Ha ha haaaa!' chortled Grandad as he and the flowers exploded through the back door. 'Did I miss a joke? Hey, here's a good one. How do you make a sausage roll? Push it down a hill!'

Mum recovered her poise quickly. 'Tea!' she announced, with fake brightness. 'Who's for a cuppa?'

'Me!' sang Grandma, arriving with customary flamboyance. 'And I'm sure Dr Atkins wouldn't mind if I had a couple of Bourbons to soak it up.'

Charlotte relaxed. No way was Mum going to reveal all—not with an audience.

She was wrong.

'The thing is . . .' Mum hesitated.

Yes? Charlotte couldn't believe it. This was like being on *Oprah*. She could almost see the slogan floating beneath her mum's nervous face: IN LOVE WITH WANNABE BIGAMIST. Her imaginary audience

200

ahhhhed in sympathy as Charlotte's own slogan sailed past: WANNABE GIRLFRIEND OF SLUDGE-EYED GINGER LOVE GOD WHO JUST WANTS TO KNOW WHAT'S GOING ON.

'*Yes?*' snapped Grandma. She didn't do suspense.

'I'm seeing someone.'

There was a stunned silence.

'What, you mean like through the window?' asked Grandad. His chair creaked as he craned his neck to peer into the gathering darkness on the other side of the glass.

'No . . .' said Mum patiently. 'I'm seeing a man. I'm going out with someone. Someone new.'

Charlotte rolled her eyes. It didn't look as if her mother or Mr Grant had done much *going out* the other night. There'd been rather a lot of staying in going on if you asked her. Unfortunately, nobody *was* asking her, so her infinite wisdom was wasted.

'He's very nice,' Mum went on.

No, he's not, thought Charlotte.

'He's very clever.'

Thinks he's clever.

'He *loves* books.'

So did Charlotte. But *she* didn't go around locking wives in attics and swanning around in Julie's Lotus while corrupting poor, defenceless, lovesick teachers, did she?

'I see,' said Grandma. Her pursed lips formed twin cushions of crossness, which were scary enough. The layer of Super-Hydrating Wild Raspberry made them positively terrifying.

'That's nice, petal,' said Grandad, oblivious to the undercurrents of disapproval that were surging about the kitchen. 'About time you found yourself a chap. What team does he support?'

'I . . . er . . . I . . .' This was so not the question Mrs Penman was expecting. 'Brighton and Hove Albion?' she ventured.

Grandad nodded appreciatively. Clearly this was the right answer.

Buoyed by his reaction, Mum faced her own mother with renewed confidence. 'You'll like him,' she said.

'Hmph,' replied Grandma. 'I'll be

the judge of that.'

'Why didn't you tell me?' asked Charlotte, unable to stop her voice trembling. She was now beginning to feel rather put out. Whether Mr Grant was a bigamist or not, didn't *she* deserve an impassioned plea for understanding? (Not to mention assurances that cappuccino and ivory silk would go perfectly with the table decorations at the wedding.) *She* was going to have to live with the heartless toerag. *She* was the bridesmaid! Swiftly, Charlotte rescued the abandoned bridesmaid dress from the back of her mind and mentally smoothed out the creases, while she waited for a response.

Mum looked really uncomfortable now. 'I tried, sweetheart,' she said. 'But you never wanted to listen . . .' she ventured at last. 'He's perfect for me, you know.'

Ha! He was, was he? Charlotte would be the judge of that. Mr Grant was going to have to jump through a lot of hoops before she agreed that he was the ideal man. Thrusting her nose high in the air, she made a dignified exit. She didn't want to hear any more.

As she climbed the stairs, an unwelcome and rather distasteful thought began to develop, like an old-fashioned Polaroid photo. She'd wished like crazy for her mum to find her own Mr Rochester. Now she had, but it was all so, so wrong. Luxurious sideburns he might have. He was tall and dark, all right. But the secret wife was all too real. And where was his brooding, timeless appeal? His rough charm? Without these, Mr Grant was a cardboard-cut-out Rochester.

And who'd want one of those for a stepdad?

CHAPTER TWENTY-THREE

Against all odds, the grandparents lasted until the Thursday of half term, when an almighty row blew up about the best method for trifle decoration— something to do with hundreds and thousands staining the creamy topping.

By mid-morning, they were on their way, Grandad casting an apologetic grimace over his shoulder as he obediently humped luggage down the path in Grandma's floral-patterned wake.

'See you soon, sweetheart,' he whispered to Charlotte, before they drove away at the supremely sensible speed of 27mph.

Mrs Penman was curiously unmoved by their departure. Now that she'd unburdened herself of the news about her new man, she seemed much happier. She tried to furnish Charlotte with more details, but her daughter *so* didn't want to know. So, instead, Mum spent far longer than Charlotte considered socially acceptable for anyone over the age of sixteen giggling on the phone. And never had anyone looked so eager to go to a crusty old book group that Friday night. Either Mr Grant was going to be discussing *War and Peace* with them or Mum was aching to discuss her new beau with the literary types at the bookshop.

'Let's do something fun tomorrow!'

205

she sang as she gambolled down the path that evening.

Charlotte shrugged. What did Mum have in mind? A cosy fireside tête-à-tête—in which case they'd have to get a chimney fitted—that would help her to understand just why her mother was fraternising with a married man?

Quite frankly, she'd rather go to a garden centre.

On second thoughts . . . while the stink of hydrangeas still lingered, maybe not. Instead, she texted a plea to Manda: WANT 2 SHOP. NEED 2 SHOP. MUST SHOP. U?

The response was instantaneous: YAY!

* * *

Friday began early, thanks to megaphone-wielding seagulls cackling wildly outside Charlotte's bedroom window. Mum had returned late, long after Charlotte had snuggled up with *Jane Eyre* and the wonderfully dull St John, or Sin Jin as everyone at the BBC seemed determined to pronounce him. But now her door was firmly shut and, as there was no way Charlotte wanted to witness Mr Grant in his PJs—ewwww—she gobbled a bowl of Weetabix and legged it to the bus stop before anyone adulterous awoke.

Boots was calling.

Charlotte debriefed Manda at the bus stop. Her best friend nodded sagely throughout, agreeing and disagreeing in all the right places.

'Yes?'

'*No!*'

'Absolutely.'

'Pyjamas?'

'Urgh.'

The 5B arrived just as Charlotte's rant was building up to a crescendo.

Manda put a finger to her lips. 'Later,' she said, before trilling, 'An all-day special, pur-*lease*!' to the near-catatonic bus driver.

Charlotte mumbled, 'Same again,' and scuttled up the stairs behind Manda to discover that the top deck was almost empty. But not quite. And, right there, right now, time stood s-t-i-l-l.

Draped across a double seat as if he were modelling the stained velour upholstery for DFS . . . was . . . was . . . Charlotte gulped. It was Jack.

Wow.

'Your mouth's open,' whispered Manda. And, when there was no response, 'Shut it before you look like a Thunderbirds puppet.'

Stunned into submission, Charlotte obliged.

'Hi,' she squeaked.

He nodded briefly, without breaking eye contact.

Charlotte went to sit beside Manda, who unhelpfully plonked her bag on the seat beside her, forcing Charlotte to sit nearer to Jack. She'd have words with Manda later. Obstruction, that's what it was. She smiled apologetically, marvelling anew at his eyes—today, green Fruit Pastilles, twinkling as if they were sprinkled with sugar. As she stared, his pupils dilated beautifully.

Oooooh!

When Charlotte had thought you could only get this churny-lurchy-gurgly feeling from a Chicken Madras, she'd been wrong.

'Yoohoo!' called Manda, neatly ruining the moment. She looked back and forth between Charlotte and Jack, who was now staring resolutely out of the window at the second-hand shops they were passing. 'Don't all talk at once, will you?'

It wasn't that Charlotte didn't want to talk. It was just that she couldn't think of a single phrase that didn't include the words 'er', 'um' and 'so'. And they were hardly going to snare her a boyfriend.

Fortunately, Manda had decided to cover for Charlotte while she recovered her poise. Already, she was treating Jack to the choicest morsels from her long-practised repertoire of Witty Facts Guaranteed To Entertain A Boy While Your Best Friend Is Speechless. She was utterly brilliant, hogging the limelight with style. As the bus chugged past the concrete 1970s eyesore of a town hall, Jack gazed unblinkingly at the one-woman show.

'I like an Aston Martin DB5 as much as the next person, but you can't beat the Bugatti Veyron for pure speed, can you?'

'Paintballing . . . now, there's a game I love!'

Charlotte began to have regrets. She'd wanted to be spared the awkwardness of a date, but in her more soft-focused moments, she'd seen herself cutting into the conversation with the odd pithy phrase. Maybe a gag or too. Now all she wanted was a gag— and perhaps a length of gaffer tape—to stem the relentless flow.

On and on and on . . . Manda paused only to grimace at the ticket inspector as he examined her ticket, before swivelling back to her captive audience of one.

In the millisecond that eye contact was broken, Jack took his chance. 'Are we there yet?' he pleaded, directing his question at Charlotte.

There were three stops to go before the town centre, but before she could reply, Manda had jumped in again. 'Nowhere near,' she announced. 'Did I tell you about the time I went bungee-jumping backwards?'

'Yes!' snapped Jack. He sprang to his feet as the bus slowed. 'I've er . . . I've . . . that is, I'm going to—' In too much of a hurry to finish the sentence, he swung himself into the stairwell and slithered downwards, out of sight.

'Manda!' hissed Charlotte. 'What have you *done*?'

Her friend frowned. 'Exactly what you wanted me to do,' she said. 'Remember? We've discussed this so many times . . .' She puffed out a weary breath. 'I was putting him at his ease. Subtly steering the conversation towards blokey topics so he didn't feel overwhelmed by oestrogen. Entertaining him while you were struck dumb by the forces of lurve, so you didn't feel like a prize pillock.'

'But you didn't let him *speak*,' Charlotte said, with increasing desperation. 'And now he's *gone*.'

'I thought I was doing rather well, actually,' huffed Manda, pursing her lips. 'Won't bother next time.' She turned and stared furiously out of the window at M&S as the bus shuddered to a halt. Even her back looked cross.

It was only nine thirty and already Charlotte had done the triple. Manda was mad with her. Jack was scared of her. Mum was too busy with Mr *Grrrrrr*ant to give a stuff about her.

Excellent.

She thudded down the stairs and off the bus in Manda's angry wake. Wordlessly, but with much tutting on her friend's part, they headed for Boots and its aisles of wonderment, where it was possible to lose entire days. But even though Charlotte spent the entire time looking out for Jack, she didn't see him once.

CHAPTER TWENTY-FOUR

Charlotte had always believed implicitly in her own super-theory that time gathers speed during a school holiday. And if only Einstein hadn't wasted time bending space, she was sure that he'd have come to the same conclusion. By the Sunday of the autumn half-term break, time seemed to be whizzing by so fast that she barely had the chance to get dressed in the morning before she slumped back into bed again at night.

Mum was in a splendid mood. She sang 80s hits. Constantly. Duran Duran, ABC, Soft Cell . . . She was so incredibly happy that Charlotte was loath to interrupt the good humour with the boring, but ultimately necessary questions she'd lined up.

1. When is *he* moving in?
2. What about his *wife*?
3. What am I supposed to say to *him* at *school*???

Meanwhile, there had not been a single word from Jack, electronic or otherwise. Charlotte couldn't help blaming herself. If she'd been brave enough to speak to him, she could have interrupted Manda's well-meant monologue with a covert invitation to the arcades on the pier or whatever it was that boys did when they weren't looking impossibly luscious.

Jane Eyre would have done

something about it. Fearless Jane. The petite heroine with the heart of a lion. Or was that the Wizard of Oz? Whatever. Charlotte was nearing the end of her latest rereading of The Book, which meant that it was all nearly over.

Over.

Like her non-starting romance with Jack.

In despair she dropped an email to her dad, who was catching his last precious rays of the year in Brazil before returning to the UK at the end of the Grand Prix season. She didn't tell him about Mum and Mr Grant. It would make it more real, somehow. And she didn't want that. Not yet. She didn't tell him about Jack either. By the same token, she wanted to delay the realisation that she'd blown it.

Dad was his usual cheery self. 'Missed you, chuck,' he emailed. 'By the pool. Got a beer. Cool. See you next week. Let's do sushi.' She grinned. That was one good thing about having a global tourist for a dad. He would rather wear pink than go to

McDonald's.

*   *   *

It was with a heavy heart that she trudged to school on Monday morning. There were six long weeks until Christmas. Six weeks during which she'd have to run the gauntlet of Jack's goo-green eyes and get used to the idea of living with the shockingly arrogant and immoral Mr Rochester that she'd foisted on her mother.

Ding-dong merrily on blinking high.

'Sorry . . .' said Manda, falling into step beside her. 'I won't mention the bungee-jumping next time.'

'Don't worry about it.' There was no point holding a grudge against her best friend when Charlotte was so lily-livered herself.

'Penny for them?' asked Manda.

'Not worth it.'

'Hmm.' Manda raked her fingers through newly hennaed hair. 'Unlucky. That's the smallest denomination I offer. You'll have to fester on your own then.'

Charlotte sniffed back a sudden sob, the influx of cold air making her head spin. 'OK,' she said. 'No new developments since Friday. No surprise stepdads at dinner. No moonlight serenading under my window. Satisfied?'

'Not really,' said Manda brightly. 'Not until you stop moping about. *Then* I might leave you alone.'

'Yeah, right,' grumbled Charlotte, but Manda's trademark cheeriness was working its usual magic and she no longer felt quite so desolate.

Manda pulled back her sleeve and checked her watch. 'Hey, guess what?'

'What?'

'It's Monday, it's five to nine . . . and it's assembly with Miss Stone!'

'Arrggghhh!' cried Charlotte, jerked out of her romantic torpor at last. She swung her schoolbag round her head in the style of a beefy Russian hammer thrower. But Manda ducked, laughing maniacally as she sprinted between the wrought-iron school gates.

Charlotte knew something was wrong as soon as her soles squeaked onto the over-polished parquet flooring of the school hall. At first glance, everything looked normal. The teachers patrolled the perimeter, ushering pupils to their seats with a series of nods and frowns. The piano was as out-of-tune as ever, rendering 'Peer Gynt' virtually unrecognisable. (If it *was* 'Peer Gynt'. Manda often claimed that Mr Jeffries allowed the piano to remain in such a state so that he could get away with playing 'Three Blind Mice' instead and no one would recognise it.) Mrs Hook's scarlet lipstick was the same terrible, puckered scarlet. Nevertheless, *something* was amiss.

'They're smiling,' said Manda in an undertone. 'Look at them—they're all grinning like Cheshire cats. Are they on drugs? Can we get them arrested for it and banged up in a Thai jail?'

Charlotte checked out the bared teeth for herself and shuddered. What was going on? She looked at her mother, but Mrs Penman was grinning like the rest of them. If anything, her smile was the widest.

Mr Grant was the only one behaving normally. Brooding and smouldering and grumpy as ever, he sat looking determinedly at the floor. Was it Charlotte or did he look a weird shade of green? Was his rottenness revealing itself at last? Suddenly, he clasped a hand to his mouth and staggered from the hall.

The French teacher's strange performance only added to the curious chatter in the hall. By the time Miss Stone stomped up the central aisle like a small, tweed-clad bride, the excitement had reached fever pitch.

'*Good morning!*' the head teacher boomed, gripping the lectern as if it might run away.

There was a hushed silence, before the assembled pupils hurriedly chanted, '*Mor*-ning-Miss-*Sto-wone.*' Like they always did.

'I think I said "*Good* morning"?' The head teacher cocked her head and giggled playfully.

Everyone looked at each other. This was a new one. What did she expect them to do now? Repeat the new

218

phrase or reply with, *'Oh no you didn't!'* and *'Behind you!'*?

Miss Stone tittered again. 'And why, pray, is it a good morning?' she asked cryptically.

A child with pigtails fired her hand into the air. 'Because there are still fifty-six shopping days to Christmas?' she ventured.

'No.' The head teacher's scary smile wavered for a second, then came back full force. 'Try again.'

'I can't resist,' muttered Manda. And before Charlotte could shackle her, she'd raised her hand. 'Because we're *so* blessed to be under the tutelage of such an esteemed staff?' she said sweetly.

Charlotte screwed her eyes shut and waited for the inevitable counter fire. She could smell detention from here. There was a moment's silence, probably while Miss Stone loaded her virtual AK-47 and adjusted her sights.

'Correct!' boomed the head teacher.

What?

Charlotte's eyes sprang open and she gawped at Manda, who looked gobsmacked in the extreme. All around them, pupils began to mutter excitedly. Had their great leader finally gone mad? Would they get the day off to celebrate? What did 'tutelage' mean?

'I am delighted to announce,' began the head teacher, pausing as the collective sense of anticipation exceeded anything ever achieved at the Eurovision Song Contest, 'that Harraby Comprehensive has passed the Ofsted inspection with flying colours. We are officially: *Good.*'

So *this* was why everyone was so unnaturally happy. It all made sense now. There was a smattering of random claps from the Upper Sixth—who would applaud anything if there were an outside chance it would boost their coursework marks—before the teachers joined in with uproarious cheers. Manda shrugged and then added a whoop of her own. Soon the hall echoed with enough decibels to give an EU official palpitations.

Miss Stone nodded contentedly, her grey helmet of hair swaying back and forth. As the noise abated, she held up both hands for calm (or possibly in preparation for an impromptu volleyball match—the gesture was unarguably ambiguous). 'Which brings me to my next point,' she continued.

The hall quietened.

The head teacher—who had clearly watched too many reality shows over half term and was dragging out the pre-announcement pause to obscene lengths—smiled blithely at everyone. When they could stand it no longer, and even the teachers' smiles were fading, she went on. 'We will celebrate this fine achievement on Friday evening. You are all invited to a rather special school dance!' She beamed contentedly at everyone.

Polite applause rippled around the hall. Charlotte joined in with a few half-hearted claps. There were only so many times a person could cheer this early in the morning. And this was unlikely to be the last bout of clapping before they were released so she needed to preserve her energy.

'It will be fancy dress!' cried Miss Stone, with as much aplomb as if she'd just announced the Christmas Number One. 'You will all—and that means *all* of you—dress as literary characters.' A hand was raised on the front row. 'People from books, dear,' she said.

A wonderful bubbly feeling rushed from Charlotte's head to her toes. And then back again. She smiled at Manda, who jerked her eyes ceilingwards and then smirked back. She smiled at Mum, who gave her a knowing look and a wink. She cast her smile wider, skimming the hall until she encountered a pair of eyes that made her fizz all the more.

But Jack Burley was deep in conversation with a girl in the next seat.

He didn't notice Charlotte.

CHAPTER TWENTY-FIVE

'Tonight, Manda, I *am* Jane Eyre!' Charlotte twirled so her friend could admire her gloriously dull outfit. Fashion aficionados might have described it a symphony in brown: long brown skirt (bolstered with every underskirt Mum owned); brown blouse; a white cap made from butchered handkerchiefs perched on top of her temporarily tamed hair.

'Wow,' said Manda, carefully winding bandages around her neck. 'Now show me what you're really wearing.'

'You're hilarious,' said Charlotte. 'No, really. You should be at the Edinburgh Festival. Ha ha.'

Manda raised a mummified hand to secure a safety pin behind her ear. 'Sorry, very authentic,' she conceded. 'Not going to get you a snog though, is it? You'll be lucky to get a second glance looking like that.'

Charlotte raised her chin haughtily. 'Romance is *not* on the agenda,' she said. 'I am simply upholding the memory of the greatest book ever written.'

'Yeah, right.' Manda started work on her feet.

Charlotte watched transfixed as her friend slowly turned herself into a

223

mummy. 'And you are?' she asked.

'*The Invisible Man,*' Manda said smugly. 'HG Wells. 1897. Ha.'

Charlotte grinned. 'Nice one.'

Four whole days had passed since Monday's assembly. Four days in which they'd been almost unnaturally free from homework—the first time in her life Charlotte would actually have welcomed trigonometry to take her mind off Jack. Four days in which he had cavorted around school with a succession of girls. He seemed to be around every corner, either whispering in their ears or springing guiltily away when he saw Charlotte. She did what any self-respecting rejectee would have done. She ignored him totally.

The only bit of good news was that Mr Roger Grant, serial adulterer, philanderer, bigamist and wearer of unfeasibly large sideburns was off sick. He was blaming a dodgy oyster, apparently. Charlotte sniffed haughtily when she found out. It would be an oyster, wouldn't it? The food of love. Serve him right for overindulging. But at least now she was spared her aloof/grumpy dilemma of how to behave in her future stepdad's lessons.

And meanwhile, Friday had loomed closer. For once, there was universal approval for the head teacher's idea, which added a carnival-like atmosphere to break times. The dance was to be held in the school hall—now specially decorated with A1 replicas of the first pages of assorted classics. The fairy lights usually reserved for Christmas were looped across the ceiling to create a starry-night effect. Disco Dave—a great favourite at teachers' weddings—wasn't available, so Mr Jeffries had come to the rescue with his steam-powered record player and prized collection of 80s hits.

It was going to be brilliant.

Mrs Penman certainly thought so. The broad smile she'd worn to assembly remained firmly stuck to her face all week—not even a disastrous incident featuring a Year 8 pupil, a can of Diet Coke and a copy of *The Mill on the Floss* could banish it. Still Charlotte hadn't confronted her about Mr Grant, who rumour had it would be recovered in time for the dance. She would do it afterwards. There was no harm in putting it off a little longer. It wasn't that she was hanging onto their pre-sideburned life by her fingernails. Oh no.

'Are you girls ready?' called Mum. She knocked politely before unceremoniously yanking the bedroom door open to reveal a frock of supreme buxomness. 'Well, don't you two look smashing,' she announced over the top of her empire line. 'Which novel are you from, pet?' she asked the now totally mummified figure.

Manda nodded mysteriously.

'Right.' Mrs Penman turned to her daughter. 'And you must be . . . Catherine Earnshaw from *Wuthering Heights*?' She hooted with laughter at Charlotte's indignant expression. 'No? Well, perhaps Jane Eyre then. I hear that's a *terribly* good book.'

They smiled at each other, a flicker of affection passing between them. It was just like the Olden Days, before Mr Grant stepped in and spoiled things.

'Come on, then!' said her mother. 'Mrs Bennet from *Pride and Prejudice* at your service. World-class whinger, total embarrassment and taxi driver to the stars. Haven't we got a party to go to?'

*   *   *

The school hall pulsed to the ancient rhythm of *Tainted Love,* while a mildly nauseous display of disco lights swirled dizzyingly across the ceiling. The room was already packed. Frankenstein's monster swayed alongside Mr Pickwick and Harry Potter. Mrs Hook was wearing an elaborate Mrs Tiggywinkle costume and attempting the jive. The Famous Five were head-banging.

Cautiously, Charlotte stepped forward, trying not to trip on her too-long frock as she looked for a suitably inconspicuous piece of wall to lean against. She didn't want to draw attention to herself, not if Jack was unavailable. It was totally against the rules to develop a new crush when the embers of the old one were still cooling. She looked up.

There was no possibility of taking a walk that day. We had been wandering, indeed, in the leafless shrubbery an hour in the morning; but since dinner (Mrs Reed, when there was no company, dined early) the cold winter wind had brought with it clouds so sombre and a rain so penetrating, that further outdoor exercise was now out of the question . . .

The writing was truly on the wall. The very first lines of *Jane Eyre* were pinned like a great literary omen above the trestle table of dubious refreshments. Charlotte shouldn't have been surprised to see the familiar words— not with her mother on the party committee—but nonetheless she felt a shiver of excitement swoosh through her.

She quashed the feeling at once. Jack was taken. She'd be far better concentrating on being Jane Eyre rather than hankering after—as Manda so delicately put it—a snog. She scurried to the edge of the room, within eyeshot of her namesake's words, which were strangely comforting, and pushed her back firmly against the wall.

The music squawked to a halt and then Spandau Ballet blasted out of the speakers. Charlotte surveyed the room, much as she imagined Jane Eyre herself might have done. She was on the sidelines, looking in. By now, Manda was clamped firmly to Frankenstein's monster in a curiously appropriate pairing. There was no sign of Jack.

A tall, dark man with a nose so hooked that it was either moulded from Plasticine or he was seriously disfigured, marched into the school hall. A small, pretty woman hung on his arm, staring up at him adoringly.

'Roger!' cried Mum.

Ah, so it was Mr Grant beneath that hooter.

'Jackie!' It was Mum again.

Charlotte watched goggle-eyed as Mrs Bennet glided towards the couple,

229

shaking them warmly by the hand.

Er . . . what?

Had Mr Grant brought *his wife* to the party? (Charlotte had somehow assumed that poor Mrs Grant would be locked in an attic, like all respectable mad wives. Not that it was any more acceptable for Mum to have an affair with a man whose mad wife was locked in the attic . . . Yet the Grants were doing such a cracking impression of a happily married couple . . . What did that mean? Worst of all, Mum *knew* his wife, which meant she was knowingly having a fling with a friend's husband! Finally there was Julie. Julie-with-the-orange-Lotus. Mr Grant's *other* Other Woman. Where did *she* fit in?)

Charlotte stared and stared, not knowing what to think.

So she didn't.

Instead, she looked away from the smiling trio and stared dolefully around the psychedelic hall, watching everyone else having the best time. Jack still hadn't arrived, but that was hardly news. He was probably locked in a passionate embrace with any one of the hundreds of girls she'd seen him with since Miss Stone had told them about the dance. The head teacher herself was dressed mutton-lamb style as a stunningly inappropriate Scarlett O'Hara. But frankly, she didn't seem to give a damn about it.

'Jane Eyre, would you care to dance?'

'Huh?' Charlotte dragged her attention away from the dance floor and found herself staring right into a pair of green eyes. Not pond water, not wheatgrass juice, not Brussels sprouts, not avocado, not moss, not mould, not watermelon nor Fruit Pastilles. And definitely not goo. Just green. 'Huh?' she said again, stupidly. This wasn't happening. It couldn't be.

A long, utterly delicious second passed.

'Mr Rochester?' she breathed.

He bowed low.

Her heart swelled.

Was this *really* happening?

It *was*!

Right on cue, the music slowed to a leisurely swaying rhythm. Reluctantly,

231

the head-bangers slunk out of sight, grumbling loudly. And, as if in a dream, Charlotte floated onto the dance floor and held on tightly to the tall boy with the high collar and the stuck-on sideburns that were made from orange wool.

Only Jack Burley could make orange woollen sideburns look cool.

'You do like Mr Rochester, don't you? It wasn't Darcy, was it?' he checked, looking immensely relieved when she nodded happily. 'It took a lot of research to get this just right,' he whispered into her ear, as he swung her round and round. (He was a very bad dancer.)

Charlotte smiled. 'You're perfect,' she whispered back, just before his lips touched. 'Just perfect.'

*　　　*　　　*

Late that night, long after the disco, Charlotte sat at the kitchen table clutching a battered copy of *Jane Eyre*. (The less precious TV tie-in version that she reserved for moments of extreme cereal eating.) Her face ached like she'd smiled for a thousand wedding photos. Yet she was *still* smiling because it wasn't every day that a girl got to kiss Mr Rochester. Charlotte figured that she had at least another week of constant grinning to go before she downgraded to intermittent beaming.

'Ta-daaaaa!' Mrs Penman plonked a cup of steaming cocoa in front of her.

Charlotte interrupted her reverie for a second to smile her thanks.

'Now,' said Mum. 'I think it's about time I explained and you listened.'

'Hmm?' For a second, Charlotte didn't have a clue what her mother was yabbering about. Explain what? How Jack was going to get the superglued sideburns off the side of his face without removing his skin at the same time?

'I need to tell you about . . .' began Mum.

Charlotte remembered. The brightness of her smile dimmed a few watts. 'Mr Grant,' she finished.

Mum didn't flinch. 'There's never

233

been anything going on with Mr Grant,' she said in a rush. 'Honest. Honestly honest. Cross my heart and hope to die, stick a needle in my—'

'Stop! I believe you!' said Charlotte before Mum got any more graphic. 'What *has* been going on then? Did he let his wife out of the attic for the school dance?'

So Mum told her everything. It didn't take long because it wasn't that complicated, really. It seemed that Charlotte had got it all horribly wrong. Mrs Penman and Mr Grant were just friends. They'd *always* been just friends—apart from when they'd crossed swords, when they were just enemies. What's more, Mr Grant's wife was *not* imprisoned in the attic. In fact, as well as being as free as a bird and working as an air stewardess on long-haul flights, Jackie was jolly nice too. She and Mrs Penman got on so well that they had booked up for the same Italian evening course, though why a teacher would want to spend their free evenings being taught was beyond Charlotte. She decided to let that go for now.

'Julie?'

Here was where it got *really* embarrassing. Julie was Mr Grant's sister. His *sister*! Not his part-time girlfriend at all. Though she did drive a Lotus. And it guzzled petrol, which made the French teacher very unhappy.

So Mrs Grant wasn't in the attic. And Julie wasn't a scarlet woman. Which meant that Mr Grant wasn't Rochester in the slightest. Not even a tiny bit.

Charlotte smiled hesitantly. There was one more scary question to ask. She mustered all her courage and then went for it. 'And your new man . . . ?'

'. . . is the owner of Barnham's Books.'

Huh?

Once she explained, it was all so blindingly obvious. Mum had actually been seeing him all along. She'd joined the new book group so she could see more of Edward—at last, *someone* had a romantic name!—and *he* was the reason she'd been smiling so much. She didn't want to introduce him to Charlotte until she was totally sure about him herself.

'You'll like him,' said Mum confidently.

And Charlotte actually thought that she might.

*   *   *

Even later that night, long after she had switched off the lamp, Charlotte lay staring into the inky darkness. She still held onto *Jane Eyre*, but had loosened her vicelike grip now. Her mobile was within easy reach, in case Manda felt the desperate urge to contact her again. Her best friend had regretted fondling Frankenstein's monster as soon as the lights came up and texted three times before midnight to say: NEVER AGAIN and ARGGGHHH and WHY DIDN'T U STOP ME? I BLAME U!

And what about Jack Burley? Well . . . she could hardly believe it. All the time she'd been looking for a love interest for her lovely mum, Charlotte had failed to notice that her very own Edward Fairfax Rochester was right under her larger-than-average nose.

Jane Eyre would have loved him.